charlene's Angels

colingirks

CODEX

Charlene's Angels
by Colin Ginks

Published in 2000 by
Codex Books, PO Box 148, Hove, BN3 3DQ, UK
www.codexbooks.co.uk
codex@codexbooks.co.uk

ISBN 1 899598 15 4

Designed and typeset by Artery
Printed in the UK by Cox & Wyman, Reading

for Michael Langan

Colin Ginks was weaned on *Doctor Who* and electro-pop, and seemed doomed to failure. He was a struggling journalist, graphic designer and troubled heterosexual from Brighton dreaming of foreign shores. Jump ten years to Lisbon, Portugal. Ginks is a new man. Successful homosexual, a career in antique dealing behind him, he moonlights as derring-do artist and writer. *Charlene's Angels* is Ginks's first novel.

JUNE 1996, LIVERPOOL,

a summer when the sun actually shone.

European football euphoria countrywide.

'Born Slippy' on the radio day-in, day-out.

George Michael still in the closet.

Where were you?

1

THE CATHEDRAL LOOMED OVER GUS like a Nazi stormtrooper as summer heat slapped him with a sweaty paw. He banged the front door shut, breathing deep. The sun hung bloody in the seven thirty-five sky and Gus shivered with hot joy. Here he was, the Summer Boy. The Star Child, bastard offspring of Johnny Rotten and Rimbaud. He gulped down his speed, wrapped in yellow paper, and then stepped into Canning Street heading in the direction of the city. The Mersey spangled below in lilac chemical haze, the Liver Buildings glinting in its wake. Majestic. Eight miserable fucking months of winter's bitchy glare before this moment – the realisation that summer had arrived. Gus, with best mates Damon and Serge, had waited impatiently, choked like cars at bottlenecks. Fingers numb, shoved down the front of their trousers, laughing in the freezing air so sharp it had nearly spiked them. Now they knew why they had been so bloody stubborn. Why they hadn't packed it in to hustle with Pearl in San Diego. He'd begged them to join him – he was gagging for it. Serge had almost climbed on that plane; in the end, he mailed Pearl two gorgeous frocks, size 38, to say sorry sister, but this was his home now and anyway, he was chasing some cute Scally lad, number one crop, hard as a boxer, but with coy blue eyes which reminded him of the Adriatic…

A prostitute clicked her heels on the corner of Hope Street as Gus brushed by. "Do you want any business?"

"No thanks." Wasn't it obvious? His tight CUM T-shirt, bondage trousers, his hair savagely orange.

People stared at him from the sanctuary of passenger seats as he crossed the road towards Chinatown, on his way to MelloMello. Gus stared right back, even staring defiantly at the car load of Scallies in the Ford Escort Cabriolet. Summer justified his every move. The Scallies screeched by in the direction of Toxteth, wolf whistling, but they were playing Maxi Priest like stupid heterosexuals and Gus felt infinitely superior. He liked Super Furry Animals, 60 Ft Dolls and Marion. He also liked Gina G. He was in control.

Damon had said that Gina didn't win Eurovision because of the Greek Orthodox block vote. High camp was way over their heads. He should know; second generation immigrant from Thessaloniki. His mum had the broadest Scouse accent this side of Scottie Road, though the stink of feta cheese on her plump fingers gave the game away. But she was alright, Damon's mum. She was the only one to accept them when the three of them came out together at 6pm on Thursday March 13th, Gus's birthday. His dad hit the roof and Gus hit the streets. It was really nasty. He spent a couple of nights on Charlene's couch before she found him a top floor bedsit on Canning Street, which he loved. Here he was able to dream up radical manifestos in peace, or play the Jesus and Mary Chain loud without dad raging. He so wanted dad to see him now, sorted. He'd written his phone number on a 'Wish You Were Here' postcard and sent it home, but they never rang. Never.

"What do you think of him then?" Gus craned his neck towards the bar where Damon's new boyfriend was buying a round. Black leather bomber jacket, white Fruit of the Loom T-shirt, tendons dancing in the back of his neck. "Not bad. Who is he? Where'd you meet him?"

"He's Jonny." Jonny lifted his leg onto the foot-rail and they watched his arse tighten. Gus winked at Damon appreciatively, who blushed and smiled. "He works at the local sauna. He hands out fresh towels."

"You sound dead keen."

"Be'ave! We only met on Saturday night. He had his hands under the blowdryer in the toilets at Baa Bar. Nice hands.

I started chatting to him about Shearer swapping his shirt after the Scotland match. He looks a bit like Alan Shearer, don't you think?"

Gus looked up at Jonny as he returned to his seat with two rum and cokes and a bottle of Becks for himself. Strawberry blonde short curls, a hard face that broke into a soft, open smile as their eyes met. Not bad at all, Gus thought. Damon pinched Jonny's bum as he sat down and said, "Thanks mate. This is me friend, Gus."

Jonny squeezed Gus's hand and gave him a peck on the cheek. He smelt of Cool Water. "Alright? Damon said you're learning to be a DJ."

"Uh-huh. I've stuffed chickens, fried mad cow burgers and stacked shelves. Then I dyed me hair and never looked back."

"Me brother DJs at weddings. He's straight like," said Jonny.

"Not exactly Cream is it."

"Jonny's out to all his family," said Damon. "They're really cool about it."

Jonny nodded. "Everyone knows about me in Old Swan."

Gus eyed him up, the boy next door with the confident, masculine gestures and a voice so deep you could dive into it. Gus felt a bit jealous of Jonny. People would accept him on whatever terms; his aura danced between straight and gay. Gus, meanwhile, had yet to even accept himself. He wondered sometimes, staring at his naked reflection in the full-length mirror of his bedsit. His body was soft but strong enough. Nice, smooth cock – he was thinking of piercing it. He would play idly with the ring in his left nipple and remember as a boy making daisy chains, hiding his broken teeth under the pillow, but always laughing... When had it all gone strange?

He looked over at Damon, those green eyes rapt in the heady spectacle of his new lover. Damon always fell in love. His heart was pure mush. Gus and Serge gave him so much stick about his appalling taste in men. And he never seemed to get the hang of it, always left stranded when the last bus went home. But this time, Gus had to admit, it might be different. Jonny was their age, quite a catch in a fuck-you-on-spit-behind-the-bike-sheds way, and he seemed to really get off on Damon. He was stroking the dark hair on Damon's forearm, licking his finger and making little crop circles. This time, Gus didn't feel the need to shield his friend. Serge always told him, "You're too soft on Damon and too hard on yourself." Gus felt he would get round to himself eventually, he just didn't know when. Perhaps now that Damon seemed all coochy-coochy with a fella that hadn't stepped out of the *Rocky Horror Show*, Gus really had no excuse.

"Alright lads?" Sharma planted a hot kiss on Gus's cheek, threw herself onto the sofa next to Damon, and shouted across to Paolo behind the bar to mix her a Bloody Mary. She ruffled Damon's tousled hair and motioned towards Jonny. "And whose are you?"

"Hands off, he's mine," said Damon, his cheeks reddening. "Jonny, this is Sharma, our bitch with balls."

"Watch it you! Charmed Jonny – you can shampoo my carpet any time."

"Well I–"

"Katy Ann, get here will you!" screamed Sharma over Jonny's embarrassment. From behind the bar a Robocop doll emerged, guns blazing. A little girl's voice squeaked, "Blam! Blam! Blam!"

Sharma stood up, her body jewellery clattering against her Gaultier bodice. "Get out from behind there and say hello to the boys!" A tangle of black ringlets framing almond eyes popped up between the bar pumps. "You have 20 seconds to comply," added Sharma.

Katy Ann was top-to-toe like her mother in black end-of-the-millennium streetwear. Their eyes locked combatively; gun-metal sparks flashed. Sharma's heavily made-up stare bore into her daughter's. Katy Ann put up a fight but eventually looked away. Sharma could outstare anyone. Katy Ann scrambled resignedly onto the bar before leaping to the ground revealing My Little Pony knickers mid-air. She landed firmly on her purple DMs. Gus pulled Katy Ann onto his lap and hugged her. "How's my favourite Indian princess?"

"I'm not a princess," she said with a look of disgust, "I'm Jubilee."

"Have yer seen the *X-Men* this week then?" asked Damon.

"Yeah, it was brill. Xavier and the Beast got frozen by Magneto, and Storm made the sun come out and melt them."

"Was Gambit in it? I really fancy him."

"Don't be giving her any ideas," butted in Sharma, "I want her to grow up to be a lesbian." Completely ignoring the surprise etched on Jonny's face, she turned to her mates, "Are you seeing Serge tonight?"

"He's not out," explained Gus. "He's had a new tattoo done and it's not healed yet."

"Charlene gave me a letter for him. You know what she's like. I saw her for about two minutes between hair at Toni and Guy and a breakfast TV shoot. She said she could have left it on the table at home but Serge is hopeless."

"The only thing he notices is cock," agreed Gus. "This letter," he asked, trying to sound casual, "is it from his family?"

"Looks like it."

"I'll give it to him, if yer like," offered Gus quickly. "I might go and see him later."

"OK," said Sharma, somewhat reluctantly, handing over the letter from the confines of her bumbag. She carefully watched Gus pocket it. "Make sure it doesn't get mysteriously lost."

"Who's Serge?" asked Jonny.

"He's our Action Man."

"Our big-dicked bodyguard," added Damon.

"Ex-mercenary, Bosnian refugee, big fan of East 17 and totally queer," said Sharma wistfully.

Jonny swigged from his Becks, trying hard to take it all in. Damon had made a point of preparing Jonny for the gallery of dead-gorgeous rogues and misfits who were his friends. "How'd he end up in Liverpool then?"

Gus cleared his throat and began, "As with many things in life we have to thank Charlene. She was in Sarajevo—"

"Sarah who?" interrupted Jonny, looking bemused.

"Sarajevo," continued Gus irritably, "you know, the Yugoslav civil war." He rolled his eyes at Jonny's evident unfamiliarity with current events. "God!" he snorted. "One wonders why I get so disillusioned with homosexuals. Show me a queer that can see further than the end of his nose ring."

"Eh!" protested Damon, nudging Gus sharply in the ribs. He turned towards Jonny and snuggled contentedly under his chin. The others rolled their eyeballs in unison.

"Eurch! You two are hanging!" groaned Gus. "Well if I may continue? Bosnia was a Yugoslav province until the recent civil war in which it thrashed the Serbs and got independence. Charlene was in Sarajevo when the hostilities broke out. She was the British delegate for the Transsexual's International Tribunal and Streetparty – TITS for short. They were holding their annual conference there when the bombs started raining. The hotel they were staying at – being of course the most glitzy in the whole province – was a prime target and took a direct hit. Serge pulled her out of the rubble, took one look at her and confessed his queerness. His mission for the Bosnian freedom fighters was to get insider information on cross-dressing. Transexuality was considered the perfect disguise should their attempts to overthrow Milosovic fail. Anyway, he and Charlene swore allegiance to each other there and then on the spot. She told him if he ever got in too deep and needed a refuge he should come and stay with her in Huskisson Street." Gus sucked furiously at his rum and coke and Damon continued, "Three years later – last November in fact – Charlene's doorbell rings and there is Serge, standing at the door on the verge of collapse."

"No!" gasped Jonny.

"Yep. It turned out that Serge had had an affair with a Serb marine and they were discovered by his commander shagging in a torpedo bay. Serge got away – his lover wasn't so lucky." Damon made a cutting motion across his throat.

"No!" Jonny's voice was now barely a whisper.

"Apparently," interrupted Sharma, "he escaped over the mountains with Serb shocktroops not far behind. He managed to get away and eventually to Paris where he slept rough for a few weeks before stowing away on Eurostar. He tried hitching after that but no one would pick him up, he was in such a state. So he walked all the way along the hard shoulder of the motorway until finally he got to Wavertree and got a taxi from there. Charlene nursed him back to health in total secrecy for a month before introducing him to us all on Christmas Day last year. That was a present and a half I can tell you!"

"Christ!" exclaimed Jonny, leaning back in his seat and opening his legs.

"As good as," said Damon. "Now him and Charlene are as close as mother and son. It's dead touching really, how protective they are of each other."

"A dead gorgeous Yugoslav in the 'Pool? I'd like to protect him given half the chance," said Jonny with a grin. There was a brief, awkward silence and Jonny was aware all eyes were upon him. Damon pulled at his arm and threw him a quick warning glance. Jonny felt the air around Gus's body bristling.

"Serge'd have yer guts for garters if you called him Yugoslavian to his face," muttered Gus grimly. Oops, thought Jonny, better change the subject. "How come I don't know Charlene?" he asked quickly as Damon put his hand gently on his inner thigh. "Everyone seems to have some story about her."

"Shut yer fat gob!" hissed Sharma, placing a finger to her mouth. "That's one person you don't ask too many questions about."

Damon smiled reassuringly at his boyfriend. "She plays her cards very close to her size 40C chest," he said. He looked around furtively before whispering darkly, "You might remember her as Charlie Monroe – y'know in her 'past life'."

Where had Jonny heard that name before? He wracked his brain in search of the relevant memory cells, but to no avail. Damon's hand sliding delicately up and down his leg brought him out of his reverie as he felt the warm shifting of his balls. Jonny spread his legs wider to accommodate the growing muscle in his red Champion briefs. The slight discomfort only made him feel hornier and he sat up to make an adjustment. "Allow me," said Damon who deftly put his hand down Jonny's dark blue Diesel jeans. Jonny groaned and bit his lip. "Don't. You'll make it worse." Smiling he took Damon's hand by the wrist and slowly withdrew it, pressing it to his nose and kissing the fingers. Gus couldn't help but notice the clear, glistening liquid on the tip of Damon's thumb. He felt quite jealous – he couldn't help it. This letter for Serge – *his* Serge (even if he didn't know it) – had made him feel insecure enough already without wanton displays of sexual electricity in front of his very eyes. Deep down, Gus felt that Damon had found Mr Right just to spite him.

"Mum! Mum! Come and look!" Katy Ann had jumped off Gus's lap and was pressing her nose against the glass looking out onto Slater Street. Lime neon burned in her jet-black hair. Night was finally crawling down over the rooftops. Sharma and the lads looked towards the commotion bubbling up behind the now darkening window. A mass of indecipherable heads bobbed at eye-level, while another soundtrack from outside mish-mashed with the bar hubbub. "Let's go see!" Katy Ann wriggled between the seats and tornadoed out of MelloMello before her mother could lay an orange-fingernailed hand on her. "Fuck!" Sharma swore savagely. "I should have that little bitch on a lead." She leapt up in a rage of zinc and leather. "C'mon. I might need you boys."

Slater Street, a disturbed stew of opposing cultures: fish'n'chip suppers and tapas, Irish shanties and Alex Reece. God knows how it had stayed on speaking terms this long with its mad-for-it Scousers, pretentious students and coachloads of Cream clubbers. They crashed into each other like dodgem cars from bar to bar, but always having a laugh. Bleached dolly-girls in fluorescent skirts halfway up their arses, tottering on thick white platform heels; Scally lads in short-sleeved Ted Baker checks talking drunkenly to apprehensive lurexed faggots. The scene was ripe for disaster – black-clad bouncers eagerly willing a bloodbath to ease their pent-up aggression – but somehow it remained elastic and sinewy and ultimately human in its scale. Liverpool was out on the streets and you'd have to look pretty damned hard to match it for sheer bloody-mindedness.

Shadowy figures darted across a makeshift sound system that loomed over the crowd like marauding slabs of liquorice. Dressed in Nikes and Stüssy baggies, they looked around furtively, nervous of their success. They worked rapidly, each completing their task and slipping back into the shadows. Clumps of power cables that snaked down from a flat above Tito's bistro were thrust into the speaker innards. The ground shook with the surge of power that spat up hot gravel.

A bottle green Vauxhall Astra found its exit blocked, marooned in the flotsam and jetsam of boozers, ravers and the merely curious. The driver stared impassively through thick bifocals at the mass of bodies pressed against the car's flank, his window rolled up tight. His hand was glued to the horn, but he was completely ignored. He watched a wing mirror disengage and drop to the ground. The vehicle rocked from side to side with the swell of people. A little girl in purple DMs climbed up the bonnet onto the roof. It was Katy Ann. She sat down, legs crossed, rocking back and forth. She watched with breathless glee the mass of bodies around her frugging to a low, insidious bassline. "Uncle Gus, is this a rave?" she squealed as he lifted her onto his shoulders. "You just hold tight Jubilee!" he shouted above the drum and bass and deafening happiness. He stood in awe of the spontaneous emotion welling up, wreathing the rooftops in sublime madness.

Gus beamed at a hobo who had unwittingly found his way into the jumble of spun-out bodies. He clutched a half empty bottle of designer vodka to his coat, fiercely afraid of losing it. "Wicked mate!" yelled Gus. The homeless man nodded vigorously and then added hopefully, "Can you spare us some change please?"

Jonny saw a mate of his brother's whom he had once slept with, dancing with his girlfriend. All three exchanged broad grins as Damon pulled him along into the mêlée. "Fuckin 'ell Jonny, this is wild!"

"Brilliant," whispered Jonny, "fuckin' brilliant." Damon turned and studied Jonny's face wildly, that ice-cream complexion melting into blueberry eyes. He really wanted to kiss those smooth crimson lips. Damon even thought he was in love. Not the desperate physicality of loneliness that speared his softness, no, this was raw, sweet-pained and Damon was deliciously afraid. His gaze caught Jonny full in the face – "Give us a kiss." Jonny did. Damon's legs nearly gave way under him.

Sharma caught up with Katy Ann and Gus. A clutch of Czech football supporters stumbled between them, commiserated in defeat by this display of western hedonism. Their blue painted faces shone like fish scales as Sharma shook them vigorously by the hand. "I'm made up!" she spluttered. "Welcome to Liverpool." She added slyly. "Sorry your crap team got thrashed. Come on Katy Ann!" Her daughter landed nimbly on the ground and they moved hand-in-hand into the throng. Gus laughed and as he ducked to avoid a loose swipe at his head, he caught Katy Ann's almond eyes flickering with orange light. Weird. For a moment he thought he was having a bad reaction to the speed. Wrong. The beams of a police van's headlamps swept across the back of his neck. Two vehicles screeched to a halt at the crowd edge, trussed up with thick mesh as though ready for war.

The crowd looked edgy and started to pull back. For a moment nothing happened; all froze in expectation, ignoring the phat beats booming from the speakers. The vehicles sat there, full beam, illuminating the nervous faces of the multitude. For want of something to do, a bloke shouted, muffled, "Fuck off pigs!" and launched a beer bottle at the Transit vans. It exploded against the mesh in a fizzy ball of gas. It triggered the police offensive. Armour-clad figures poured out in unison from the vans, raising truncheons over their heads. They let out a roar, like B-movie savages in the wrong scene, and rushed the front line. It was crude but effective. Gus saw people scatter in blind panic. The Czechs' blue faces became spattered with red as the police laid into anyone who strayed into their path. Truncheons and bats crashed down onto cowering bodies, hands raised to protect their heads. A stricken tranny, tangled in her hairpiece, was on the receiving end of a vicious blow, teeth ripped from her gums in a bloody fountain.

Dodging projectiles launched from behind the makeshift barrier of the bottle green Astra, the police quickly reached the sound system. They formed a ring around the speaker mountain and punctured the sleek felt with the end of their truncheons. The music screeched in agony. One b-boy, upon witnessing the flagrant desecration of his gear, pulled a homemade spike on a chain from the folds of his puffa jacket and advanced, whirling it over his head. The police line fell back. "Come on!" screamed the lad. "Are you chicken? Come back here you fuckers!" He let the weapon fly indiscriminately, whereupon it meteored across the rooftops before crashing through the window of a nearby stationery store. The clatter of an antiquated alarm added to the cacophony as amused Scallies dipped into the shattered Parker Pen displays.

The driver of the Vauxhall panicked and reversed blindly, careering into a lamppost and smashing a tail-light. The rubbish bin clamped to the concrete stem of the streetlamp was ripped off, scattering sodden chip papers skyward. Gus saw a copper demobilised by a fatty newspaper sheet that glued itself to his visor. He pulled in panic at the headline obscuring his vision. Half a dozen ravers pounced, kicking him to the floor, beating the shit out of him. The car narrowly missed flattening his head as the driver put his foot onto the accelerator and weaved through the battleground. Gus turned in slow motion to see Sharma and Katy Ann just manage to dodge the car and escape into the relative safety of a greasy spoon. Katy Ann was bawling and trembling as Sharma spat abuse at a passing helmeted copper. "You fascists! You fucking fascists!" and then she too burst into tears. What's going on, thought Gus? Why are they doing this? Everyone had been having a good time, on his or her best behaviour. Now furious, provoked, the ravers sent empty beer bottles and whatever else came to hand flying over Gus's head. They smashed against the advancing line of Perspex riot shields, the policemen batting them away like in some surreal baseball game. Inexplicably, an ancient Tomahawk chopper bike soared across the sky and knocked down a line of policemen in a slapstick moment. Other officers stepped on and over them, gradually, brutishly, viscerating the crowd from the inside out. Gus was rooted to the spot, caught in the middle. A youngish-looking copper who had lost his helmet and had found himself on the wrong end of a bottle of Grolsch, spotted this orange haired boy standing alone. He made for him, thinking, "You fucking no hoper, I'll show you." He smacked him across the side of his skull and Gus went down. He felt as if the whole of his head had collapsed inward as he crawled towards an alleyway across gumdrops of broken glass. He lay down and looked up at the night sky, the noise from the riot ringing in his ear. He put his hand to his head and felt the sticky wetness on his scalp. Blood. He licked it.

"Gus!" Two figures emerged from the dark. "Gus mate! Are you alright?" Damon and Jonny took one arm each and pulled him to his feet. Gus's head boomed. He groaned. If I try to speak, he thought, I'll throw up. "I think he'll be OK," said Jonny. "Let's get him home."

"No," said Damon, "we'll take him to Charlene. She'll look after him."

"Those fucking bastards!" cursed Jonny.

"Yeah, bastards," echoed Gus feebly.

"Come on, hon," whispered Damon softly, "let's get you cleaned up. It won't be the first time I've put you to bed on a Saturday night."

"I suppose this is what it feels like to be a dizzy queen," mumbled Gus.

"Sshh," said Jonny. "Save the camp wit for later."

They pulled him onto debris strewn Slater Street, carpeted with broken glass and discarded platform shoes. The police were shoving a few stragglers into the back of another van. The boys saw a girl, her dress torn down the back, being handcuffed roughly before being shoved by the arse from one copper to another. They laughed brutishly at her distress.

"What happened to your mate then?" A square, thickset policeman faced them, tapping his truncheon casually against his thigh. "Oh nothing," said Damon, dangerously sarcastic, "he just got in your way, that's all."

The policeman took a step forward. "You're a queer, aren't you? Get out of my sight, you fucking faggots, before I do you over." He brandished his truncheon leaving Jonny and Damon in absolutely no doubt as to what he meant.

"I want to go to Charlene's," said Gus wearily. "Please let's just get out of here."

Jonny brought a black cab screeching to a halt and, as they lifted Gus into it, Damon felt his stomach tightening with anger.

2

A BIG FAT RIVER wallowing in its muck like a slug. Bound by wide flats of slime, it heave-hoes with the consistency of hot chocolate mixed with spit. Packet boat ferries chop into its spume, satisfying beleagured tourists in their primeval need to go and come back with a telephoto snap at halfway point. In spite of Heritage Walks and Magical Mystery Tours, the river weaves its enduring spell. The Mersey: watery stuff of legend. Thank the Beatles for that, probably. Or maybe Frankie. Or, more obscurely, the African slave trade. Few remember that, the blood on which Liverpool built its fortune. Here, Scouse merchants grew fat on the grisly trade of vacuum-packed misery between Africa and the New Improved Continent, glittering on the heavy Atlantic horizon. Watered down legacies – the Mersey does this, even today. It washes away sins on flaxen tides, leaving a faint poisonous residue, faint bloodstains on the black tarmac.

The city uncoils slowly, meaner as it distances itself from its greedy river and the dirty laundry soaking in the swell. The thrust of Georgian stone in the commercial centre impresses first, chocka with happy shoppers resisting the lure of the mall in an accent seemingly weened on helium balloons. Newspaper vendors catcall, *"Echo! Echo!"* in the thrill of the latest slapdash headline of Major's health cuts. Shellsuits battle it out with drab student grunge in a circle around the insane 'Nessun Dorma' karaoke, performed by a City fan to enthusiastic applause. Plastic shopping bags flap busily in the wind tunnel.

Behind the escape valve of Bold Street, the antique residential interlace digs its heels in, straddled by Liverpool's two obtrusive cathedrals. They taunt each other from opposite ends of Hope Street in a characteristic display of Scouse tetchiness. Here Charlene's Angels scrabble for air amongst the eclectic brew of aspirant *meejah* professionals, faggots and home county undergraduates, while Toxteth threatens to spill over into their back yard. Cappuccino fur-lipped, bookish types brook the occasional celebrity in the Number Seven Café on Falkner Street, seeking civilised haven from the antagonism. Nevertheless passing Scallies scowl at them on the way through to the contaminated artery that is Princes Avenue.

Deceptively genteel street scarring the 'Pool's hide; its tall facades of stuccoed opulence cannot obscure the flagrant, voluptuous decay that wreathes the rooftops. Its daytime, sunlit spell is bright enough. Aged Jamaican gentlemen, with grizzly silver beards, cogitate serenely from the grassed central reservation as taxicabs clatter by like black beetles. Explosions of coloured saris wreathing petite Indian women pull a train of bushy-eyebrowed children whooping excitedly in broad Scouse. However, by the small hours the innocence has wisped away. Shadows rise from the hideous housing estates flanking Princes Avenue and now the real fun begins: aggro, vandalism, blood feuds between warring clans in the rush to control the dark city belly.

Bouncing baby Charlie Monroe debuted here, found lodged between the yellow pages in a brick-red telephone booth on a freezing fog night. A pretty boy, wispy curls, his eyes swallowing hungrily the grim, destitute tableau of post-war, post-great Britain. Hanging limp on barbed social policy, he was shunted from one Catholic orphanage to another abusive warden with the customary Establishment zeal. Insipid, unstable males finding legitimacy in the young minds and bodies of disconnected, dysfunctional youths – Charlie may have been among the few to enjoy it. After all, it fired in him the warped fascination for terror, and for cruelty, that precipitated his make-over to end all make-overs.

Charlie Monroe's story was carried on blustery winds, in one ear and out the other, blown across the front page, through the now-derelict dockland of his teenage years, out to the river. His is a story rarely told these days, superceded by Cup Finals and child killers and Brookie. It skimmed the oily river surface, whooshing over Charlie Monroe's supposed resting place beneath its murky depths. Going, going, gone.

The Mersey serene, washes out to grey sea, and Liverpool is granted another reprieve.

Gus woke to the sensation of a hand stroking his face. It muffled the dull thump that still inhibited his brain. He buried his head into the pillow. "Thanks for last night," he murmured. "I always seem to land on your doorstep when I'm in trouble. I guess you're getting sick of the sight of me by now."

"Silly Billy. You know Charlene loves you."

Gus recognised the unexpected voice and lifted his head. Serge. Regarding him intently, dazzling eyes, long lashes. A smile playing on his lips. Gorgeous bastard. "Oh. I thought you were Charlene," he said awkwardly.

"Really?" said Serge, amused. "I never saw myself as tranny. You think I look good in a dress?"

Gus clutched his head. "Serge, I'm sorry, save the laughs for another time. I had a run-in with the boys in blue who decided to use me for target practise."

"Charlene told me," said Serge, slightly put out. "What were you doing, anyway?"

"Would you believe me if I said I was just standing there, minding my own business. Fuckin' police state we're in."

"Fucking state you are in, it seems to me," Serge remarked drily. He placed a finger on a nasty looking weal on Gus's shoulder. The battered boy winced. "You play too rough, I think," admonished Serge. An idea came to him. "I know," he grinned mischievously, "just relax. I'll make you a nice massage, make you better."

Gus panicked, "Oh, I don't know if that's such a good idea…" Somewhere within a little devil gagged for it.

"Oh shut up," said Serge, "I don't want to hear another word of you." He affected a come-to-bed voice. "Now lie still and take it like a man."

Gus slowly rolled onto his back. "I bet that line comes in useful," he puffed, as his war wounds accommodated his new position. He opened his mouth to venture some other sarcastic remark, but was stopped short as Serge whipped the bed sheets from over his bum crack in one deft movement. "That's better," he heard, and was too caught by surprise to disagree. His heart waited for permission to beat.

Serge began to stroke Gus's back, gently, but firm. He worked his strong paws deep into the root of Gus's tension, located somewhere between the small of his back and his cock. Firm pressure traversed his spine and scampered along his buttocks. Despite the gnawing pain across his skull, aching ribs, and the awful taste in his mouth, Gus got a hard-on. He squirmed slightly to press it between the mattress and his belly, but Charlene's cool satin sheets just made it worse.

"Where's Charlene then?" Gus tried to sound offhand.

"She left early," said Serge. "Things to do, people to see, you know?"

"Uh-huh." Gus felt himself sinking into raw pleasure, as Serge's fingers lingered down below. Suddenly, the pummelling ceased.

"Do you want breakfast?" asked Serge abruptly.

"Yerr… please." Gus looked up. "What's the matter?" he asked, noticing a strange flicker in Serge's gaze.

Serge took in Gus's bruises and cuts. "I… worry about you," he blurted out.

"You worry about *me?*" This was the last thing Gus expected to hear from Serge. He cleared his throat awkwardly, "I'm okay."

"You always say you okay and I never believe you. I'm your mate Gus – why don't you talk to me?"

Gus met Serge's gaze stonily, offended by the offer of friendship. "I wouldn't know where to start – *mate.*"

Serge pulled back. There was a moment's silence that neither wished to break. Feeling he had overstepped the mark, Gus tried to strike up conversation again. "Can I see your tattoo, then?" he asked apprehensively. Serge nodded curtly, "Uh-huh." He turned around and pulled his T-shirt over his head. On his left shoulder blade was a small, brightly coloured hummingbird in mid-flight. As the sinews of Serge's back rippled and twitched, its wings appeared to flutter backwards and forwards. The skin around it still flared red and tender. Gus lifted an arm to touch it and then changed his mind. Serge's skin was hard and soft and smooth, vaguely almonds and olives. Best not, thought Gus, my dick might explode.

"What do you think?" asked Serge.

"Very nice. What is it?"

Serge dropped his T-shirt back over his body. "Very funny. Charlene was crazy when I show it to her."

"That doesn't surprise me. You can't fart without asking her permission, can you?"

Serge's expression clouded. "That isn't true!" he protested, rather too quickly. He looked to Gus like he wished to say something more – and thought better of it. "Now, what do you want for breakfast? Eggs, a bacon, tomatoes?" Serge blanked out: Gus had seen *the change* before and recognised the doors closing on this particular subject.

"Just an egg. Scrambled, on toast." He admitted defeat.

"Certainly *modom.*" Gus smirked, wondering where Serge picked up these things. "With tea, modom?"

"Yeah. Please. Five sugars, remember."

Serge disappeared into the kitchen. Gus could finally roll onto his back and give his dick some air. As the kettle boiled in the background, he tried to recollect quite why he felt so shitty. Jonny and Damon had managed to prevent him from throwing up in the taxi while the cab driver effed and blinded at his bleeding over the upholstery. Finally, they arrived at Charlene's who tied the keys to her flat onto the end of a shocking pink feather boa and lowered them out of the window. "It was a spur of the moment thing darling," she said to Damon as he handed them back to her rolling his eyes. "The closest thing to hand." She was introduced to Jonny who gaped in awe at this six foot two transsexual in a hairnet and kimono. Charlene had, of course, taken it all in her stride. Calling Serge from his room she told Jonny and Damon to go and get some sleep and that they would look after him.

Charlene had undressed Gus tenderly as he swayed, concussed. He was certain, nevertheless, that Serge had been in the room with them and that really pissed him off. OK, they'd seen each other naked before, but those memories were anything but sweet. He wasn't confident about his body like the others were – especially Serge who had plenty to be confident about – and he squirmed at the thought of Serge standing over him while he was helpless as a babe. During their brief, abortive relationship – all 17 hours, 35 minutes of it – Gus and Serge didn't even cop off once. Well, they had slept together but had not had sex, despite the fact that Serge was a bloody nympho – you didn't dare bend over in front of him. Yet with Gus it was just cuddles. Maybe the timing was wrong. Maybe Gus was plain abnormal; he must be the only guy to be buck-naked with Serge and just get a pat on the back. Gus worried that his attractiveness disappeared with the Vivien Westwood trimmings. Not forgetting the arrival of the first letter from Bosnia, leading Serge to announce that he didn't think it a good idea if he got too close to anyone in England in case he had to leave in a hurry. Great start to the love affair of the century, thought Gus ruefully. Now Serge seemed to have relegated him to the Second Division of Shags; he barely got a look in.

Serge came back into the living room carrying a tray of steaming tea and scrambled eggs. He glanced down and caught sight of Gus's semi before he could pull himself up in the sofa bed. Serge tutted.

"What a bag of shit you are looking, darling." Serge's Slavic accent hesitated over the syllables, reminding Gus of one of those speaking Fisher Price toys he had as a kid.

"Thanks a lot." Really, Serge was spending *far* too much time in Charlene's bad company. "For that, you can run me a bath." God, I must look awful, he thought to himself.

"Well, eat first, like a good boy." Serge perched himself by Gus's side and picked up some scrambled egg with a fork. "Open wide please." Serge fed the quivering yellow fluff into Gus's mouth and he chewed half-heartedly. "Nice?"

Gus nodded, rolling the egg across his tongue. It tasted peppery with a dash of Worcester sauce that piqued his tongue. Gus sucked in his cheeks, aware of Serge observing him intensely with a faint smile playing on his lips. He felt like a little kid being spoon-fed, hair unkempt, full of lugs – this scenario was peculiar and strikingly familiar, horridly aping some childhood shard of memory. Gus cast his mind back. In the magic of his stupor, Serge's face morphed into his dad's. After the initial surprise, Gus let the hallucination flow. He was eight then and in a right state. He had come off the top of the slide in Sefton Park, yes that was it, and fractured his shoulder. "Go on lad, have a good cry," dad had said. "It bloody hurts, doesn't it?" That was the only time dad had let him cry. Tears were for poofters.

Stick-insect arm tight in a sling, Gus was ferried back from hospital with strict orders to rest and recuperate. Mum worked shifts and since dad was laid off from the docks, it was his responsibility to fix their son dinner. The only thing dad knew how to cook was scrambled egg. He had brought it up to Gus's room whilst the boy convalesced on a diet of *Silver Surfer* comics, listening to S-Express on his record player. Without a word dad had started to spoon gloops of egg into the boy's mouth, fingers smelling of hot buttered toast. Gus remembered the hair on dad's arms and the veins on the back of his hands. The same hands that had slapped him around and thrown him out only a few months ago.

Gus smarted at the memory. That's my problem, he thought, I'm looking for someone just like my dad. The trouble is, I fucking hate my dad.

He was brought back to reality by Serge asking him why he was crying, and Gus realised there was wet on his face.

"Am I crying?" he said. "Nah, don't be daft!" He wiped away the salty trails on his cheeks. "Don't pay any attention to me," he said quickly, "your company's not that bad."

Serge looked at Gus in consternation. "Come on Gus. What's the matter?"

"Nothing some blow can't fix." Gus tried to sound cheerful. Perhaps now he should hand over the letter from Bosnia that grew tatty at the bottom of his satchel. He decided against it. Serge would find out for himself soon enough, as soon as Charlene got back from God-knows-where she had disappeared to. He and Serge might spend all their time winding each other up, but to Gus this time was exquisite, precious. He pushed away the fork laden with scrambled egg. The taste was too violent on the tongue. "Serge, that was lovely, but I don't think I'm hungry. Do me a favour? Fix me a gin fizz – just to wash it down."

Serge regarded Gus disapprovingly. "With breakfast?"

"It's not when I start that you should worry about, it's when I finish."

Serge trailed his tongue over his lips. "Maybe I have one too. I like you when you are drunk – but not *too* pissed. It's... charming, I think."

"Charming? That's a laugh. I couldn't even charm the pants off meself, let alone anyone else."

Serge winked at Gus as he walked off. "We'll see, OK?"

Gus rubbed distractedly at a bruise on his arm. Serge was immensely annoying when he flirted. You'd hear wedding bells and the next minute he's chatting up some other bloke as though you didn't even exist. Gus had been through that enough before to have learnt his lesson. At least in theory – in practise it was difficult to not be putty in his hands. Gus pinched himself; he wasn't going to be such a pushover, not this time.

Serge had insisted on washing Gus's back in the bath when the phone had rung. This gave Gus time to arrange the soapsuds over his cock before Serge came back. He cursed the permanent erection whenever he was in Serge's company.

"That was Charlene. She ask how you are."

Gus grimaced, "I hope you told her, to quote your words, that I look like a bag of shit." Serge giggled and dabbed a fluffball of foam onto the end of Gus's nose. "Geroff!" the boy whimpered, before Serge dunked his fringe into the water. "What's she up to then?" Gus licked at the soapy droplets that trickled down his face.

"Charlene? Stuff…" said Serge vaguely. "She comes home after bedtime. She is on the telephone till very late sometimes."

Gus tweaked his unpierced nipple absent-mindedly. "Do you think she's still involved in dodgy stuff, like in the old days before…?"

"Gus," Serge interrupted, "she is your drug dealer. What do you think?"

Gus noticed the irritation that underlined Serge's reply. "What's she done to wind you up?"

"Nothing, Gus." He winced as Serge bent him over his knees and began to lather him vigorously. "Be a bit careful, eh?" he grumbled. "You're not in the army now."

Gus dropped his head onto his knees and hugged them to him. Serge dipped his hands into the bath water and the bar of soap slipped out of his grasp. "Oh dear," he said, as it whooshed under the thick bubble bath foam like an Exocet missile, "lost the soap. Don't move."

He rolled his sleeves up to his ample bicep and plunged his arm into the water. Gus quivered, not daring to say a word. Serge swished his arm around. "Not here."

Fingertips played lightly on Gus's arse, before reaching around to his lap. He nearly skyrocketed. A hand clutched his erect penis. "What's this? Maybe this is it?"

Gus, with an enormous effort, kept his voice steady. "The soap's by me feet. Touch me again and I'll bite your hand off."

Serge huffed, "Spoilsport." He clutched at the soap and began to swoop across Gus's back, frothing up pearly bubbles that popped in his face. A forced silence descended again, felt keenly by Gus who kept his head bowed. Serge was distracted, feeling horny and pissed off with Gus for being so prissy.

"I remember, I did this too for my mates in my army," he puffed. "Lots of fun in the showers." He contemplated the arc of Gus's bruised shoulders, resembling uncannily the damaged naked flesh of his fellow soldiers in Bosnia, all jostling for space in the communal baths. In the creamy vapour, their skin glittered endless shades of purple contusions and ruddy scars. Serge couldn't help the erection that pressed against his underwear at the memory.

"The way you describe it," winced Gus as Serge pummelled him carelessly, "it sounds more Club Med than civil war." At Serge's reticence, Gus pressed on, "Come on, you never have really told us what it was like."

"What's to say?" rebuffed Serge. He pressed his fingers into Gus's left shoulder blade. "Uh oh − I see a big zit. Keep still."

Gus felt a pain dig into his epidermis before his skin erupted. "Ow! You bloody sadist!" Through gritted teeth he added spitefully, "Charlene told me you were deflowered in the army."

"De-flowered?"

Gus groaned. "Oh it would be now that your perfect English fails you," he said sourly. "Deflowered. You know. Broken in. Played fetch the stick." He rolled his eyes at Serge's evident confusion. "Oh Lord. Fucked good and proper up the arse. Do I have to draw a diagram?"

The colour drained from Serge's face. He looked at Gus dumbly. Razor-sharp memories lacerated him suddenly, when he thought he had managed to forget.

"It's funny," continued Gus, oblivious to Serge, "I always thought you the top-heavy type. Maybe that goes some way to explaining why you're such a bastard." Pleased with himself, he had raised his eyes to gauge Serge's reaction when he was shoved face down into the slimy bath water. He gulped on a mouthful of soapy froth, which hurtled down his throat on a wave of nauseous panic. His body tensed. He tried to raise himself and couldn't – he felt the grip that secured him apply extra pressure and force his head between his legs till his crown banged onto bath bottom. He struggled. His arms batted the enamel wildly, the motion booming in his submerged eardrums. His feet scrabbled at the plughole to get a hold as the last vestiges of air in his lungs were sucked up. His innards cramped in protest. His vision blurred; everything melted into nothing as his head was held firmly underwater. His nasal passages fizzed, evacuating. He splashed a bit, ineffectually, and then gave up the exertion quite gratefully. It was too tiring for its own good. He felt lightweight, drifting in a perfumed Body Shop soup. In his head, the roar began to ebb away. Curiously, he was slightly aroused. His groin filled with blood. The hair on his legs tickled his nose as he cocked his head to the left and he almost felt like laughing. He heard music rattle in the recesses of his mind – he could have sworn it was Culture Club, 'Do You Really Want to Hurt Me?' It was too late to have an opinion on that question, really. How long had he been underwater – hours? Too long. Instinctively, Gus knew what came next, and he calmly braced himself.

He was yanked skyward in a brilliant flash of motion. Air whooshed down into his lungs like corrosive acid, sparking a vile choking fit. His vision swished left to right and around before merging into Serge's familiar silhouette, who regarded him fixedly.

"You – fucking nearly killed me!" Gus spluttered.

"No I didn't," replied Serge steadily. "You just – talk too much sometimes."

Gus forewent all modesty and stood groggily in the bath. His prick bounced incongruously like a kangaroo. His hands groped empty air. "Get me my towel!" he slurred. Behind his temple his head thundered. "I don't fucking believe it!" was all that Gus could articulate. He saw himself in the mirror and he had gone an alarming blue colour from his chest upwards.

Serge handed Gus a rainbow towel from last year's Pride and he wrapped it around his shivering torso. Serge began to rub him brusquely through the fleecy cotton. Gus flinched. "Do not touch me!" he yelped.

Serge shrugged. "OK, I don't. But no hystericals, please."

"Yer what! I couldn't fucking breath down there, in case you hadn't noticed! I'm not a bloody tadpole!"

Serge began to look a little nervous. "You won't tell to Charlene?"

"Tell Charlene? I might just report you to the fucking police! See if they can catch a real criminal for a change!"

"I'm sorry," mumbled Serge none too convincingly.

Gus bottled the hot depression rising in the pit of his stomach. Beaten up and nearly drowned in 24 hours – what did the world have against him?

"Like I really believe you!" he spat. "Just leave me alone Serge! Don't you know when you're not wanted?"

Serge glanced down at Gus's cock which seemed to wave cheerily from its bed of dark pubic hair. Gus hastily pulled the towel tight around his midriff, smothering his erection. Single droplets of water sploshed noisily off the end of Gus's stiffy into the tub. He glared furiously at Serge.

"OK Gus," Serge backed down first, "I will go in the lounge." He struggled for words to explain his behaviour. They weren't forthcoming. The blitz of shock-horror memories had receded, leaving just a prickly sensation across his scalp. "I – I just don't want to talk about – stuff, alright?" Serge turned to leave, eyes glued to the floor. "I *am* sorry." He shut the door behind him.

Gus exhaled slowly. The back of his throat still burned. He rubbed his swollen windpipe gingerly as he swung his legs onto the bathrug.

Unravelling the towel around his waist, his penis bounced enthusiastically back into view. Gus moaned in despair. Spitefully he pinched the flesh of his testicles; it hurt, but even that felt nice. He gave up – it was ultimately reassuring that at least his dick worked properly, if anything too well. All else was a big, steaming mess of cosmic proportions.

His reflection confronted him from the steamed-up mirror. Gus barely recognised his own likeness, picked out in rivulets of moisture. It was physically knocked out of shape – *really* attractive – but it wasn't that. He was bothered by something else. What he saw and what he felt inside had little in common. His reflection seemed to cower under his scrutiny, reluctant to make any sense. He studied himself, carefully, trying to solve the puzzle.

As they stepped into the road a sickly cloud of car exhaust fumes smothered them, stifling the White Musk bubble bath that tingled across Gus's shoulder blades. Serge gripped onto Gus's arm as the boy stumbled over the kerb.

"Are you sure you OK?" asked Serge in consternation. "I think it's big mistake you go home tonight."

"No, I'm alright. Spend the night with a psychopath? I don't think so."

Gus wavered unsteadily as Serge let go. In the dying sunlight his face was a mess of vivid colour, his eye a weeping ball of angry flesh. He hated his vulnerability laid bare. Gus wished he'd got Serge's attention without having to get his sympathy.

Serge tried to lighten the mood. "I thought Gus always wanted a gorgeous guy to look after him."

Gus wasn't having any of it. "Don't kid yourself, mate." He winced as a tender muscle protested bitchily on his back.

Witnessing this, Serge brought his hand up to Gus's cheek. Gus recoiled from the fleeting touch. "Jesus Gus, I don't hurt you!" Serge pursed his lips in irritation.

No more than you already have, thought Gus. He bowed his head as they walked on in silence. The air was still, giving them both the space for contemplation. Serge was concerned about Gus – but was just as afraid to indulge him. He knew Gus loved him; he wondered how deeply he felt too. Fantasies of Gus would catch him unawares when he least expected: on the bus, in Tesco Metro, in the shower, when he wanked. But the mangled flesh and blood reality, mooching along beside him sparked nasty, volatile side effects. Serge believed that if he could keep a hold on his past, then maybe he would come through. But Gus's fierce affection took away that control, bouncing off the barriers that Serge erected, weakening him, reminding him that a heart beat raged in his broad chest. "This is stupid," he said suddenly, "maybe we shouldn't see us any more."

Gus halted in his tracks and met Serge's gaze with his good eye. Anger glittered. "Oh yeah? How's that then?"

"I cannot be what you want, Gus. Find a nice guy, eh? Better than me." Serge edged closer. Gus could feel his breath hot on his cheek. "I fuck around. I hurt you – and I don't want to."

"Oh yeah, that's big of you." Gus turned away from him. "Fine. Let's not see each other then." Serge reached out under the amber flicker of a faulty streetlamp to pull him back into his arms. "Hey…" Sadness and sudden lust collided in Serge, deep. Gus pulled away.

"Fucking leave me alone! Don't do this to me, alright! I've been fucked over enough for one day. I don't need you messing with me head too, you bastard! *Bastard!*" Frustration erupted within Gus as he lunged at a startled Serge, knocking him on the mouth with a half-clenched fist. The blow bounced off Serge's jaw; he crumbled under its surprising accuracy. Tripping clumsily over his feet, he ended up sprawling on the pavement. His head bounced erratically on his neck, momentarily concussed.

Gus looked in amazement from his fist to Serge, struggling to get up. He hadn't expected to be quite so successful. In fact, he had kind of hoped Serge would knock some sense back into him. He watched blood trickle from Serge's split lip and stepped back. "You're cut," he whispered, half in dismay, half in awe.

Serge climbed to his feet, wiping at his chin with the back of his hand. "Ow." He shook his head to see if it rattled. "I'm okay," he muttered, chastened. The sight of blood excited him.

"I didn't mean it, really…" Gus reached out and pulled Serge's hand away from his chin. Serge seemed to open up to him suddenly, exquisitely fragile. Gently, Gus wiped away the blood that dripped slowly from the cut. He bent forward and kissed Serge tenderly. The salty taste burned on Gus's tongue and he looked into Serge's eyes. It was all the invitation they needed; they dived into each other and Serge brought his arm up around Gus's aching shoulders. Their tongues interlocked and they pulled closer, nestling together their stirring members, hungry for satisfaction. Gus's spine was bent over backwards as Serge devoured him, snagged on barbed desire. The spontaneous intensity scared the living daylights out of them both. They wanted more, yet they were afraid of themselves and each other, afraid as to where this could lead. Just as quickly as they came together, they pulled apart, nervously. Serge coloured. "Invite me for coffee?"

Gus saw the confusion in Serge's grey-green eyes and he suddenly felt perverse, triumphant. "I thought we were gonna call it a day?" He affected Serge's thick foreign accent. "I deserve better than you, wasn't it? Besides, you always said I make lousy coffee."

Serge tried to laugh but the clammy evening air suffocated the sound. "Maybe this time you do it right?"

Gus shook his head. "No, I'm off to the Job Centre first thing. Maybe some other time." He tingled with stubbornness – yet he couldn't believe he was turning Serge down.

"Oh. OK." Serge gingerly approached Gus and kissed him on the cheek. It glistened in the neon flare. Serge raised a paw and softly stroked the side of Gus's face. Gus flinched. "I'll give you a ring then."

Serge stepped away. He felt something whizz past his ear. Then, metallic, it clanked at his feet. He looked down onto a scrunched up beer can. Gus stared upwards, confused, and Serge spun around. Wolf whistles from a third floor tenement, two lads hanging out from an open window. "Fucking queers!" gurgled one. The other laughed. "Arse bandits!" Another can came hurtling down, this one half full. Beery foam sprayed up onto Gus's combat trousers. He stepped back uncertainly. "Get going Serge, eh?" He slipped into the semi-darkness.

"Fuck off, you faggots!" spat one lad, his voice thick with deeper venom. Serge grimaced, hands on hips, standing his ground. They stared down at him. "Next time I see you, I'll slit your throat from ear to ear," the one demonstrated with drunken brandishing of the imaginary blade, "carve my name on your fat faggot's arse."

Serge turned around wearily and walked away, immune to their taunting. As he approached Charlene's flat, he could still hear his aggressors drunkenly mauling Oasis's 'Live Forever.' Wankers. Country full of fucking wankers. The words curled deliciously around his mind and Serge wished he could spit them out in elegant, complete sentences. Instead he was always awkward, tongue-tied. A faggot's greatest weapon is his tongue. Serge turned his key in the lock. It caught, finally, with a protesting metallic rip.

3

JONNY JAMES LIVED THE FRAYED REALITY of inner city depravation and bulldozed dreams, yet he always smelt clean and fresh scrubbed, even after footie with the lads from next door. He had wanted to be a striker for the Reds; those strong calves and size seven feet in symbiosis with the ball fashioned miracles from thin air. Jonny was a Scouse cliché: tough little bugger with a gazelle's grace on the pitch. Now ligaments and sinew jostled with metal pins at intervals along his right foreleg. Memories of sudden snapped bones, hot summer tarmac sizzling, cooking blood as it spurted eager onto the spinning wheel of his upturned motorbike. The machine protested like a wounded bull. Jonny knew better than most how precarious dreams could be.

NHS counselling filled the void of training practise. Rehabilitation; community reinsertion; social reassessment. Average schooling leading to average employment. Family loving, supportive, strangely ineffectual. Jonny raging, he found consummation in a public lavatory on a day trip to Wigan Pier. As he shot cum over the older man's face he let out a howl that brought the day to a standstill – from then on he knew how to channel the pain.

The neighbourhood let him be, let him desire its husbands and builders glistening on distant scaffolding; hadn't he suffered enough, for being a good lad? In fact, Jonny gained a sort of mystique – the local girls fancied him even more, lads in shell suits sought him out at the pub. Jonny stuck it out at home with quiet stoicism, believing his pops needed him. He was probably right – he was the dreampool in which they had dived and drowned. His tragedy ridiculed them all, one way or another.

Despite the unspoken regrets, the family pulled together, perhaps as much out of habit as desire. Strange and yet so common that behind the dreary one-dimensional simplicity of inner city lives, lurk intricate psychotic webs, binding souls in hurt. The Jameses were no exception; they demanded nothing and got it back in spades, always laced with disaster. Like today for example, a day like any other. Jonny was watching basketball on Sky Sports, stroking his crotch absent-mindedly through his tracksuit bottoms. His cock responded semi-erect, alerted by the lanky, hot bodies on the flickering screen.

Johnny's head, though, was elsewhere. Damon danced in his mind's eye; in fact, Damon kind of stamped on each and every thought as if they were bugs. For Jonny, the intensity of the intoxication was scary. He wondered how Damon reached the parts that other queers could not reach. What made him different to all the other blokes he had copped off with that year? Some of them were fitter than Damon, like that Geordie with the tattoo on his butt. Jonny counted all the way to 12. Thirteen if he included that fella he disturbed wanking in the bog at Lime Street Station...

The doorbell rang. Jonny peered through the soiled net curtains at the figure standing on the doorstep, mopping his sweaty brow with a spotted handkerchief. Jonny's heart skipped a beat. He shrank back as the man flicked a beady black eye on the swaying curtain. Crouching out of sight, Jonny switched off the telly.

Jonny shot through to the backyard, piled with rotten rabbit hutches, snagged plastic, a lifetime's debris. Ma sat there in a blue floral dress, catching the late afternoon sun, bouncing little brother Jason on a fleshy knee. Jason gurgled contentedly, spiritedly waving a plastic raygun; ma sang Mungo Jerry and wiped his grimy face with her spit.

"Mam," puffed Jonny, "there's someone at the door. I think it's that fella. The one dad owes all the money to."

Mam's reddened face drained of all colour. "Christ, son." She heaved herself out of her deck chair, Jason falling to the ground. "C'mere baba." The little boy huddled in her thick arms. "Jonny, what we gonna do?"

"I dunno mam."

The doorbell rang again a second time, a finger pressed down hard on the button so that it repeated its electronic chime frantically in a never-ending loop. Mrs James emitted a low whining sound in the back of her throat. "Jonny, get me stick from the larder." She stroked Jason's soft, mottled hair. "Door mam," said the boy, pulling at her skirt.

Jonny found the stick amongst the ancient, dusty cartons of Bird's Custard Powder and jelly squares. A thick heavy oak cane with a gnarled end. He felt its weight in his hand and his heart shuddered insanely in his chest cavity – it could make a nasty mess of someone. God forbid that he should be forced to use it. He emerged from the larder and mam looked at him fearfully. Jonny tried to smile reassurance, "I'll keep hold of this."

"Let's be careful love." Mrs James was wringing her hands together all the while. Jonny motioned for them all to keep quiet.

The doorstep silhouette shimmered behind the frosted glass as they edged uncertainly towards the front door. Continuing its piercing catcall in overdrive, discordant notes corrupted the doorbell's banal tune. Mrs James pushed Jason back; he hung at her thick legs. The figure, detecting movement, took his finger off the bell and suddenly swooped. Nicotine stained fingers poked through the letterbox. A voice, high pitched Mersey, squeaked, "I know you are there Mrs James. You'll make things a lot easier if you open up."

Mam pulled Jason into the polyester folds of her knee-length skirt. She tried to disguise the quiver in her voice. "I'll not do anything till me husband's here."

A beady black eye surfaced letterbox level. "I think your husband's made enough of a mess of things, don't you?

Why not open up and we can talk it over like decent human beings, eh?"

Mam glanced at Jonny who shrugged uncertainly and gripped tighter onto the stick behind his back. As Mrs James edged the door open, the inner city burble of traffic congestion and screaming infants bounced off the walls. The man was scrawny, beak-nosed, smothered in an oversize charcoal suit which failed to disguise his puny frame. He affected a smarmy grin which stretched his nostrils across his face, but his eyes darted warily from side to side. "Thankyou Mrs James," he winked. "All I want is a little chat." He saw Jonny. "Ah, I see the cavalry's arrived."

"Just tell us what this is all about," said Mrs James, quickly.

Beady eye man whistled incredulously. "I can't believe you've forgotten already. Last time around we had such a nice afternoon, you and your husband, me and the boys. Remember?"

Jonny looked at his mam in alarm. He knew nothing about any visit. Mrs James's breathing rasped like clogged drains. Beads of sweat twinkled on the end of her ruddy nose. Angry energy prickled across Jonny's bare shoulder blades at the sight of her suffering. "Mam…"

"Shoosh love." Mrs James's voice shook perceptibly as she stood her ground. "You're just going to have to come back another day," she pleaded. "You can't just turn up unannounced and expect me to have your money for you."

Beady eye man sighed. "I can see I'm wasting my time. My fucking precious time." His face twisted into a snarl as he darted over the threshold. "Maybe this will help speed the process up a bit." Two hulking yobbos, dressed in black, emerged from next door's garden.

Mam let out a shriek and pushed in panic at the door. The intruders rammed it and spilled into the hallway. Jonny felt light-headed as he raised the stick above his head. "Hey, get back! Take one step closer and I'll knock your fucking block off, I will!"

Jason raised the toy gun and began brandishing it at the bruisers towering over him. One looked down and, sporting a warped grin, lunged at the little boy. Mam screamed and retreated behind Jonny, yanking the wide-eyed Jason with her. "Baba, go on and wait for us in the backyard. We'll play with you in a minute." She gave him a gentle push away but Jason installed himself at the kitchen threshold, hanging onto the doorframe. He watched them all intensely, sucking at his thumb lodged firm in his mouth.

"Now listen here," said mam defiantly, "like I've told you, me husband's not here. When he's here, I'll get him to give yous a ring. I promise."

"Empty promises, Mrs James. I've heard it all before. All the excuses under the sun. We've been patient and we haven't seen a single penny from you. That's very serious, Mrs James. You owe us a lot of money. It's hardly fair that I go out of pocket just 'cos you can't be bothered to get off your fat arse and pay your dues, is it?"

Mrs James choked back a sob. "Please – just leave us alone."

Beady eye man shrugged his shoulders indifferently. "My heart bleeds for you. It really does. But business is business." He motioned his thugs forward. "You know the score. If being nice doesn't work then there are other methods at our disposal."

Jonny brandished the cane wildly. "Back off! You heard me mam. Dad's not here. There's fuck all anyone can do."

"You're an annoying little cunt, eh?" Beady eye man winced as the stick cut air inches from his head. "Alright son. You've had your say. Now just put the stick *down.*"

"No fucking way! Not till you get out." Beyond the edgy thugs, Jonny could see a crowd of neighbourhood onlookers forming. He stepped forward, wanting blood. "Go on, piss off! You try anything, you'll have half of Old Swan after you."

Beady eye man threw a look over his shoulder at the ever-growing group of locals staring grimly back at him. "Listen laddy, do you have any fucking idea what you are dealing with here? This isn't Toytown and I definitely am not Noddy." Pleased with his analogy he grinned, a twisted slant to his bony chin. One of his men was reaching into his pocket for something, and seeing this, he shook his head, motioning to his men to clear out. He looked around airily. "Quite a nice set-up you have here. Wouldn't it be awful if some terrible accident happened to this place?" Turning as if to leave, he directed a kick to the bottom of the door, connecting with a glass pane that shattered into a million jagged shards. Mam screamed, bringing her hands up to her face. Jonny stepped forward but halted abruptly when beady eye man stabbed a yellow finger at eye level. "You're playing with fire sonny, I hope you realise that. You're just lucky you caught me on a good day or I'd have you strung up like a bloody chicken." His gaze shifted to Jonny's mam. "Tell your husband I want me money or bones'll start being broken instead of glass doors. No softly-softly anymore." He scuttled off with a snarl.

Jonny slammed the front door shut, which dripped glass trails from its splintered frame. The rest of the bottom pane splished down, carpeting the doormat with silver nuggets. Jonny trembled, swallowing the hot emotion that threatened to erupt. "I'll call the fella down the road to get the door fixed."

Mam leant against the wall and began to sob; Jason stared and the tears started too. "Eh... eh mam, what's all this about?" Jonny cradled his mother in his arms, rocking her softly. "It's over. They've gone now."

"Till when Jonny? When will I get another knock at the door, eh?"

Jonny's brow furrowed. He bent down to Jason's eye level and wiped away the boy's tears with his shirtsleeve. "Show mam what a big fella you are, eh?" Jason nodded, snot snivelling.

Jonny talked quietly, head bowed, stroking his brother's hair. "Tell me then, mam. Don't lie to me now. How much does dad owe this guy?"

Mam juddered down till she squatted on the stairs, hands pulling nervously at her wispy hair. "About eight thousand quid."

"Jesus Christ." Jonny felt his head ache. "How?"

"We couldn't pay the mortgage, son. The bank was threatening to repossess…"

Jonny sank down into the stairwell next to her. He knew how much dad slogged his guts out at the car plant to meet the overheads. It mortified him to have nothing but love to give to his kids when, these days, a Sony Playstation mattered much more. He was maybe too ashamed to see them for the good lads they were, giving, searching.

Jonny let out a deep breath. "I know mam. I've got one and a half thou in the bank you can have. Then Joe should have quite a bit of dough from his deejaying. That should be a good three thousand covered."

Mam rocked disconsolately on her haunches, her stare fixed into empty space. "Mam, snap out of it! Someone's gotta do something for fuck's sake!" Jonny immediately felt guilty for his outburst; pain and shame jostled for space in mam's expression. He swore at himself under his breath for his insensitivity.

"Hello? Is everything alright in there?" The next door neighbour, Mrs Mhekebeli, peered cautiously through the shattered front door.

"Come on in," called out Jonny. "Maybe you could fix me mam a cuppa while I see about getting the door fixed?"

Mrs Mhekebeli stepped in gingerly, surveying the scene of devastation. She put a hand to her mouth on seeing Mrs James collapsed on the stairs. "Lord help us," she exclaimed. "Let's get you on your feet again, shall we?" She bustled over and began to pull at the collapsed woman's shoulders.

Jonny took the steps two at a time up to his bedroom to find a T-shirt. Molten adrenalin coursed through his veins – he wished he had knocked that fella's block off. Teach him a lesson. He imagined himself beating that ugly head to a bloody pulp. He resented the way his family took each knock with muted resignation. Weaned on the welfare state that was suddenly whisked away in full-throttle Thatcherite spite, they crumbled, along with the bricks and mortar of the desolate urban landscape he knew as home. Each week a household was bulldozed, repossessed, sucked dry, to make way for the void. Yet Jonny knew that all he wished for was an out. He felt a hypocrite – but who really would want to live like this?

As he pulled a cotton T-shirt over his head, he saw Jason watching him thoughtfully from the door. Jonny grinned cheerily at him. "What's up? Cat got your tongue?"

Jason stared intensely up at his big brother, not saying a word. Jonny grabbed him and hugged the squidgy soft body tight.

"Jonny?"

"Yup, trouble?" Jonny pinched Jason's cheek playfully.

"When the nasty man comes again, are you gonna be here to stop him?"

Jonny's heart plummeted like a lead weight, down deep. He tugged a flap of skin almost spitefully as he let go. "Don't be daft! 'Course I will."

Damon turned down the football, spinning in England's slaughter of Holland. Four-fucking-one! Shearer semi-naked on the screen now, velvet physicality, arm raised high in triumph to reveal his pit of black hair beside his chest sheen. Damon supped greedily at his Grolsch. He felt euphoric, horny – and ultimately irritated, for being alone.

The telephone tempted him from amongst a heap of old college textbooks. He eyed it groggily and picked up the receiver. Jonny? Nah. Damon feared giving too much too soon like some lovesick puppy. Gus? And give him an excuse to take the piss? He shook his head emphatically and rang another number.

"Mam?"

"Hiya son." Her voice betrayed the lick of one too many glasses of sherry. "Saw the football, eh? Fab!" Damon grinned as her Greek accent threatened to swamp the painstakingly acquired Scouse mannerisms.

"Not 'alf! Dad's made up, I bet."

"Wore himself out with all the excitement. He's asleep on the couch." Mam paused, sensing deeper motives in her son's phone call. "Everything alright son?"

Damon was silent; it made her panic a little. "What is it love? You're not in trouble for thieving again, eh?"

Damon's heart raced. He struggled to find the words to express his feelings. "I'm in big trouble this time, mam. I'm – in love."

He heard mam curse as she dropped her empty glass on the parquet. "Howzat? Who's the lucky fella?"

"You don't know him mam. I only met him last week." Damon realised how ridiculous that sounded. "But it's for real," he added hastily. "I think about him all the time." Then sulkily, "I dunno what he thinks."

"Have you spoken to him about this, love?"

"Not really mam. You know, things are going pretty well. I don't want to scare him off…"

Damon waited as mam kicked dad into activity, demanding a top-up of sherry. Then gently, in his ear, "Is he nice, son?"

Damon pictured Jonny as he'd left him in his bed this morning, stretched naked across the mattress. Hair slightly flattened on the left side, dimples and face serene. Shoulders broad and soft pink, muscles cascading to the small of his back where blonde down shone, crowning his tight butt. Then when Damon had got back, Jonny was already gone, the bed neatly made. A single red rose lay on the white cotton pillow.

"Mam, he's quite a catch. His name's Jonny. Looks just like Alan Shearer."

"Good God. Has he got money too?"

"Nah, he's poor but dead gorgeous."

"Bugger! I always wanted you to marry into money, you know? Your dad was bloody hopeless." Damon heard his father muttering belligerently in the background.

"Oh *mam,* give it a rest, eh?"

"Sorry love, I just want you to be happy, that's all."

"I know. You remember telling me how scared you were for me when I came out, that I wouldn't ever be happy? Well now I am, mam. I look forward to every day I spend with him. He's kind and considerate and I'm sure he loves me right back."

Damon could hear the emotion welling in the voice at the end of the line. "Then you hang onto this one sweetheart, for all your life's worth. Tell him you love him."

Jonny lay on his bed, staring at the ceiling. He dragged on a fat joint. He had much to think about.

The boiling kettle whistled again downstairs as mam held court with the whole neighbourhood, crowded into her kitchen. He could hear dad too, back home after a pint down the British Legion. His voice sometimes boomed beneath the floor, tired and drunken as he tried to control the collective hysteria fed on PG Tips and packs of biccies. Jonny couldn't stem his rising irritation at the flabby sideshow, but felt equally guilty for judging his parents so harshly. Mam doesn't have much of a life, he thought. Let her have her moment of tragic glory.

He fixed his gaze on the shabby off-white wallpaper that was starting to peel above the headboard. Suddenly the desire to be far, far away from this world of grime and punishment muscled in. Jonny considered packing his bags right at that moment.

Damon was never far from his mind. Cute. Sexy. Tempting. Jonny feared he was attracted as much to Damon's freedom as to his undeniably good looks. Meanwhile Damon was completely into him, and he enjoyed the attention.

But did Jonny genuinely love him? He remembered waking up in Damon's bed that morning to find him gone, just a trace of warmth and his curious nutmeg smell lingering on the bedsheets. Jonny had craved slipping his legs between Damon's own, pinning the boy beneath him and relieving himself of his aching hard-on. The loneliness of the bed at that moment had shocked him.

Nineteen years, five months and 13 days was long enough to cut your teeth – Jonny craved thrills and spills. He fantasised wild 100cc gasoline horizons, Wembley FA Cup Finals, experience beyond the clammy mist of sauna mystery. Though he loved his parents and felt fiercely protective towards them, he knew he could not express his queerness from a stinking bedroom in Old Swan, no matter how supportive his folks were. Yet he felt a right cunt for even considering pulling away at this particular moment. His parents needed him now more than ever, their little treasure.

Jonny hated sometimes that he could do no wrong. Sometimes that was all he wanted to do.

The joint burned at the back of his throat as he stubbed out its dying embers. He let the narcotic swell wash over his fears and calm crystallised within his mind's eye. He opened a window to let in fresh air.

Downstairs mam shut the door as the last visitor picked up her shopping bags and waddled off down the road. Jonny could hear the chink of teacups in the washing up bowl and the sound of mam padding heavy around the kitchen. Dad irritably muttered something that Jonny couldn't decipher. Mam's curt reply stung the air.

Jonny stood on the landing, soaking up the last crimson rays of evening warmth. He waited patiently for his parents to settle back into their routine of chip fat supper and telly. He heard dad huff and sigh before collapsing into his armchair. Mam stayed in the kitchen. The burble of *EastEnders* crept slowly up to Jonny. He nodded to himself. Then, steadily, he went downstairs.

4

"SERGE FRIGGING MIJHALOVIC! PAY ATTENTION!"

The voice, an amalgam of perfectly enunciated consonants, vowels and sing-song expletives, cut the air to ribbons. Over her pince-nez Madame Lafayette regarded her pupil frostily. Serge recoiled from her temper – it was true, he had drifted off on a tide of vivid imagery, Gus centre stage. Again.

Madame Lafayette lunged for the Silk Cut nestling in her wickerwork hold-all. Beside her, China the Pekinese growled, startled at the sudden movement. Then reassured that his ferocity was misplaced, he sunk back into his velvet chair, blinking balefully.

Irritated, Serge pushed away his copy of *A Clockwork Orange*. "Why is the point anyway? I don't understand this trendy bollocks." He congratulated himself silently on the effectiveness of his putdown. Since the incident the other night, Serge was bursting with insults, carefully rehearsed. "So tell Charlene if she can't get good books I'll be home, filing my nails."

Madame Lafayette sat back in her chair, caressing her cigarette with skinny fingers. Tiny pinprick eyes sized up Serge, glittering amusedly amongst weathered skinfolds. Charlene was right – this one was certainly feisty. Ironically though, they had gotten much further with Serge than with the handful of pretenders who had previously graced their doorstep. He wasn't the first to be picked off the streets and dragged to Madame's doorstep for special tuition. All sorts of waifs and strays had been tried and tested in Charlene's finishing school. But any attempt to distil their queer essence into anything other than a lame-brained waste of limp-wristed space had resulted in failure. The manifesto perplexed them, the books bored them; they rarely could see further than the end of their next Campari and soda. Occasionally these wasted prodigies were spotted swaying blearily in the dim shadows of Garlands or the Lisbon Bar. Cowed by their frailties, aged by their empty hedonism – they were a sorry sight.

Serge, though, was different, a purer vintage. The physicalities presented no problem. Just wash behind his ears and he already looked a million dollars. He provided a cheap, exquisite high street thrill for the uninitiated who caught a glimpse as he sauntered unselfconsciously towards Kwik Save. Therein lay his subversive power.

Psychologically though, things were a little more complex. He played hard to get perfectly, resisting the seductive sloganeering that comprised his end-of-millennium re-education. Even so, the message got through; it was noticeable in the swagger, it began to surface in the ever more frequent questioning of the straight-jacket that buttoned up Britain, swollen beer belly threatening to burst out.

Why then, thought Madame Lafayette, did she have reservations as to the legitimacy of their experiment? Sometimes she even found herself questioning Charlene Monroe's motives. Despite the ennobling dream of an army of clued-up, well-hung gay youths patrolling the streets, keeping the straights very much laced, Madame Lafayette feared that their mentor had gone too far. Serge was just a kid, barely keeping a lid on his traumatic past. It seemed perverse to pull his strings as they did, tweaking his hurt into malleable shapes.

Madame Lafayette put down her autographed copy of *A Clockwork Orange*. She felt sorry for Serge. How could he hope to understand what was in store for him if Charlene had her way? What he did know was barely the tip of the iceberg. "That's enough for today." She watched him pack his papers back into his rucksack, face set like stone. "Something on your mind?" she asked, embarrassed in spite of herself.

Serge flushed. Conflicting emotions could be seen slugging it out across his brow. "Boy trouble," he said simply.

Madame Lafayette couldn't help the smile that weaved its way across her face.

"It's not funny," protested Serge.

"You're right love, it's not." Madame Lafayette felt reassured that despite Charlene's laboratory conditions, Serge still suffered the growing pangs of any boy barely out of his teens. "Anything I can do?" Madame Lafayette coughed awkwardly. The role of agony aunt was ill-fitted, but she was willing to try anything once.

Serge looked at her quizzically. "You? No thanks. I don't want him terminated – I think. He thinks already I'm psycho."

Madame Lafayette nodded curtly. "It's just a phonecall away."

"I need to calm things down. Last time he punch me."

Madame Lafayette tutted. "Darling! I wouldn't put up with that."

"Don't worry," said Serge, "I nearly kill him in the bath too. Our love is very – physical," he added ruefully.

"Stick with it," advised Madame Lafayette. "The only serious relationship I have at my age is with my plastic surgeon. Anyway," she clipped, not wishing to appear soft, "let's not have it interfering with your homework." His expression was so forlorn that she immediately crumbled.

"Tell you what love, how's about if you borrowed my motor till tomorrow? You could shoot off to Manchester maybe, or Blackpool if you're really up for it."

Serge's eyes nearly dived headfirst out of his sockets. "Me? The Carmen Ghia?"

"That's right." Madame Lafayette laid a gnarly hand on the crown of China who sighed accordingly. "Assuming you can be trusted not to ride it up any lamp posts. One thing –

it may look good but the frigging motor is fucked at anything over 60." The same could be said of the owner, but any irony passed Serge by.

"You mean it, really?" he gushed. "Wicked! I promise I be safe!"

"You do that." Madame Lafayette surprised herself by flushing bright pink at the boy's gratitude. As he took the car keys from her, she had to deftly push down the erection that crowed beneath her dress, tucked into a pair of discount frilly knickers.

Serge still hung at her shoulder, consternation creeping back into the eternal post-orgasmic glaze for which he was legendary. Madame Lafayette pushed him along. "Shoo now," she chided, "the night is young."

"One thing," Serge blurted out, "why do I feel like I'm in practise for another war? Does Charlene think she can beat the gangs again, after so many years? And me? What am I supposed to do?"

Madame Lafayette pursed her lips nervously. "Don't be silly, you big chump."

Serge lodged his thumbs into his belt hooks with determination. "All the stuff you give me, the books, the big words, sometimes I get home and my head hurts. I feel like going out and hurt someone, to chill out." He glared at Madame Lafayette. "Is that what you want? Does Charlene want me to do the rough stuff, when it's time?"

"She just wants you to be able to stand on your own two feet," defended Madame Lafayette. "You've seen for yourself how things are hotting up."

"Yeah, thanks to her big ideas," cut in Serge. "Well maybe I should stand on my two feet now and she eff off."

Madame Lafayette broke out in little beads of sweat. "Silly moo," she smiled weakly, trying to hustle him to the door.

Serge gulped, scratching his scalp furiously. Madame Lafayette watched his Adam's apple plummet down the milky slide of his soft throat and she blanched at the quality moment.

"I sometimes think, 'Serge, you made a big mistake when you come here,'" he continued. "Charlene she helps me but I think it is now I pay for sure." Serge paused. "So when is the big day? Who will I do first?" Madame Lafayette propelled him forward. "I know, 'shut up Serge,'" muttered the boy irritably, shaking off her grasp. China began to bark at the commotion from her chair, watching the steady unfolding of the scene.

Serge pulled at his rucksack, which was slipping off his shoulders. "Yeah Charlene thinks for all of us, right?" he said, sarcasm thick in his throat. He looked up at Madame Lafayette grimly. "What about you too?"

The face before him regarded him blankly. Serge pressed on regardless. "Don't you see she uses you too? Don't think you're special. Nah – you're so busy brown-nosing to see the truth, right?"

Madame Lafayette's expression clouded over. "Stop it! I've heard enough!" She snatched back the car keys dangling from Serge's fingers. "You nasty little piece of work! You can forget borrowing my car!" A sharp nail connected with Serge's shoulder. "Alright," he said apprehensively, taking a step back. He realised he had touched a nerve. "Don't think Charlene's going to like your attitude," spat the enraged tranny, advancing sternly on Serge. He shrugged truculently. "That's it!" hissed Madame Lafayette. "You think you're so hard! I'll rip your frigging liver out!" China rose from her pedestal and observed the scene in bewilderment; he goggled at his mistress as if she were mad, before flinging herself to the floor and yapping at Serge's heels. The boy back-tracked, accidently treading on her sleek head. The Pekinese renewed her efforts, piranha teeth needling at Serge's hems. "Hey, get the dog away!" Serge began to freak out.

"China, rip his ankles off!" ordered Madame Lafayette icily, face purple with rage. Serge could feel the prickle of sharp incisors digging into his ankle. He panicked. He never liked dogs, especially the little yappy variety. He brought back his free leg and, without thinking, kicked it forward into the Pekinese's soft underbelly. The creature crumpled with a strangled snap before flying through space into Madame Lafayette's gob. China responded by sinking its snout into her nose and burrowing down. Serge witnessed the broad-shouldered tranny flop onto her back like a bright bouncy castle. "Fucking hell," he uttered, flabbergasted. Madame Lafayette was emitting all kinds of whoops and whistles as her face was relentlessly punctured, arms flailing.

Serge hopped around on the spot for a brief moment, wondering if he should help. China's back legs had made a nice dog's dinner of Madame Lafayette's exposed throat too, revealing scraggly skin beneath a ton of make-up. She moaned in drawn-out theatricality as the animal began to lick at her mangled face. Well, she was still breathing, thought Serge.

He decided against coming to her aid – how would he explain his way out of this one? Now seemed as good a time as any for a test run of his future employment as a bastard thug. Serge swivelled on his heels and rocketed out of there. He bounced off the landing and dived towards the front door as the upstairs neighbour came home after a night down the pub. "Hey gorgeous!" hollered Serge, blowing the nonplussed thirty-something a kiss as he held the door open and dived out the way.

Serge landed in an untidy heap on the pavement, limbs akimbo. The night sky rushed up to greet him. He felt exhilarated, marshmallow light. "Oh shit!" he gasped. Picking himself up, Serge exploded into a fit of hysterical giggles and ran, heading in the direction of the waterfront, not knowing where he was going.

Katy Ann was playing with a Barbie doll. She hacked at its web of golden hair. It tumbled down Barbie's shoulders, down to the floor in a waxen heap. Katy Ann's eyes glittered.

"That's nice, sort of Kylie," said Gus.

Katy Ann flipped Barbie onto her back, legs splayed. Barbie prostrate on the carpet. Katy Ann pulled off the doll's skimpy turquoise dress, down to polychrome nakedness. Then she unearthed a glassy sheet of film from her toybox; fake tattoos from the sweetshop.

Gus turned to Sharma. "What pisses me off the most is meself, y'know? I just felt so... pooffy."

"Darling, don't knock it! Take it from me. Real men buy l'Oréal. Real men read *Cosmo*. Real men don't think the G-Spot is to do with the Highway Code." She sighed and took a swig of vodka from her hip flask.

"Yeah, that's alright till you read of some poor queen beaten up and left for dead in the Peace Gardens."

Sharma grimaced. "Listen love. The world is not a nice place. There are men out there who would do much worse than call you names. I should know. I've been out with most of 'em."

"You see? I couldn't even stick up for meself yesterday. Not even a good cutting remark to bring 'em down a peg or two..."

Sharma looked at Gus's crestfallen face, his lips pink pouting, and she softened. "Alright. I've a tub of chocolate chip Häagen-Dazs in the fridge and the latest *Colt*. Any takers?"

Gus raised his eyebrows. "So what are yer doing with gay porn?"

"A girl's options for sexual fulfilment are few and far between. Have yer seen *For Women* lately? I get more horny watching *Blue Peter* these days."

"Not half! OK, I'm sold. Don't forget the Kleenex."

"Eh! Any stains on me throw and you're paying the dry cleaning bill."

Gus smiled as Sharma disappeared into her bedroom, stepping lightly over Katy Ann's doll graveyard. She was right about her dubious choice of boyfriend material. They were lookers alright, but she needed someone who could at least hold a decent conversation that wasn't about the footie or the dogs. As it was, she knew more about the Reds than most of her lays.

The phone clattered in some dark corner and Katy Ann scrambled over to pick it up.

"Hello? Uncle Gus is here. Mummy's in the bedroom." Katy Ann motioned to Gus and he knelt by her as he took the receiver. A husky voice, embittered by years of cigarette abuse, sounded in his ear.

"Sweetheart, this is Charlene."

"Oh hiya." Gus groaned inwardly. Doubtless the sight of Serge with a split lip was behind this phone call.

"Well darling, I only get to see you when you've fallen foul of a policeman's truncheon, it seems."

"Yeah – thanks. Thanks a lot." Gus didn't quite know what to say.

"I think you've been avoiding me. Serge has been talking about you, keeping me up to date at least."

"I didn't know he was that interested." Gus's voice adopted a hurtful tone. He heard the crackle of a cigarette lighter and the whoosh of smoke hurtling deep down her throat. "Darling. We are a bit bitchy this morning, aren't we?"

"I just think Serge has more to say about me than actually to me face, that's all."

"Hardly a surprise when he gets a smack in the mouth for his effort." There was a moment's silence before Charlene continued, "You know darling, we're all terribly worried about you. You don't seem yourself lately."

Katy Ann climbed onto Gus's lap and he hugged her close. Her warmth made him strong.

"Maybe bad drugs – or me time of the month," he said dismissively.

"Darling, how awful! Personally, during my period I find only industrial cladding does the trick."

Gus smirked. He had forgotten how deliciously wicked Charlene could be. How her parties always ended up with

57

the police carting off a dozen pissed-up transvestites in Pucci and torn stockings. How she had bailed him out when he once tried to blow a plain-clothes policeman after Garlands; he only got nicked after asking for a tenner if he swallowed.

"I'll give you a ring," he said. "I will. In a day or two. We'll do lunch. I just have to clear me head first. I don't know why everyone goes on about Serge. That was ages ago."

Katy Ann wiggled mutant Barbie before Gus's field of vision. "I'm playing with Katy Ann's dolls." He changed tack, "Do you want to speak to Sharma?" At that point, Sharma breezed back into the living room carrying a tray of Chablis, ice cream, soft porn and a little bag of hash.

"Pass her to me, will you love? Charlene and I are planning a performance piece at the Unity about Japanese nuns who discover lesbian tendencies post-Hiroshima. I want Charlene to be Mother Superior but she says she doesn't do nude scenes."

Gus was grateful to get away. He could feel Charlene picking apart his guilty conscience with her chipped fingernails.

"I'll see yer then," he said. "I'm off to Peter Kavanagh's later. Hot date." That was a lie. He was taking Damon's mum to a night of Greek dancing at the community centre. He was a crap liar and Charlene knew it.

"Right you are," she said, as though she hadn't heard. Gus passed the phone to Sharma, feeling thoroughly dejected. He leant over and began to roll a joint.

"Uncle Gus?" Katy Ann regarded him with a startling intensity.

"Uh oh. What have I done?"

"Uncle Gus, when you get your willy pierced, can I watch?"

"Well, I don't know, Katy Ann. Things like that are very… er, private. Anyway, favourite uncles don't have willies."

The little girl's brow creased. "Silly! Yes they do." She added slyly, "Uncle Serge says you do. So can I watch?"

Gus cleared his throat. "No, Katy Ann." He quickly tried to change the subject. "What did you do at school today?"

"We said what we want to be when we grow up."

Gus lit the joint and inhaled deeply. "So what did you say?"

"I said I want to be a lesbian."

"Fuckin' hell!" Gus nearly choked on his spliff.

"And me teacher got mad, but I told her what me mam told me and that we both thought it was very nice."

"That's my baby," beamed Sharma, putting down the receiver. She scooped up Katy Ann in her arms, who began to wriggle, giggling. "Give us that, I'm dying for some…" Gus handed her the joint.

"Jesus Sharma, you're dead serious about this dyke daughter stuff."

"Bloody right I am. Katy Ann deserves better than some sweaty gorilla with no manners."

"Sounds like most dykes I know."

"Watch it! I'll give you a swipe if you're not careful!" Katy Ann rested serenely now against her mother. Sharma stroked her hair softly.

"But don't you think you're projecting some sad lesbian fantasy of yours onto her, when all she wants to do is play hide the thimble with all those little boys at school?"

"God forbid! No, Katy Ann's a dyke. She knows it. I know it. Ever since I used to breast feed her and that look on her face told me she was getting more out of it than just a fresh pint of milk. Now, if it's so bloody obvious, why fuck up her sexuality with all this boy-meets-girl crap?"

Gus supposed Sharma was right. He sat back pensively as the drugs took hold, his cock stirring under his vintage bondage trousers. He wore no underwear; he liked to feel his member rub on the zip seam.

"So how's yer love life?" he asked distractedly.

Sharma looked up at him, grimacing as she inhaled on the spliff. "Pretty crap. How's yours?"

"Friggin' marvellous. Me and Serge have officially come to blows. That's when those fellas got involved."

"You and Serge?" snorted Sharma. "I thought you'd given up that one long ago."

Gus was surprised at the sudden urgency in Sharma's voice. "Yeah well, river deep, mountain high," he said drily. "He can't keep his hands off me." Gus rubbed gingerly at his throat.

"Well I think you should cut your losses, step aside gracefully and let someone else have a go."

Gus raised his eyebrows as he took back the joint and sucked deep on its fire. "Who do you have in mind?" He saw an undefinable expression settle on Sharma's face and it clicked. "Good God – no! You?"

Katy Ann, nose crinkling at the thick cloud of dopey fumes hanging over her head, slid off her mother's lap. "Mummy thinks she's in with a chance 'cos she heard that Serge had been with girls."

"It was me that told her that, but he soon saw the error of his ways." A big grin cut Gus's face in half. "Sharma…"

"What?" She looked at him disgruntled.

"Yes, stick a paper bag on your head, quit shaving your legs, bend over and bob's yer uncle," hooted Gus. "But really! I might not be getting very far but even I'm way ahead of you, darling!" He paused and looked serious. "You do realise if you do, in fact, get anywhere with him I shall be forced to kill myself?"

Sharma laughed, embarrassed. "Don't wet yerself. All I've done is ask him to dinner tomorrow night."

Gus clapped a hand to his face. "Oh God this is bad. He doesn't stand a chance."

"Yeah well, let's drop the subject shall we? When I've got him staked out, we'll talk. And don't you go telling tales to Serge if you see him."

"Fat chance of that," said Gus ironically, "not even our lawyers are on speaking terms at the present time."

"Good." Sharma rubbed at the razor burn that throbbed beneath her leggings. "So you think, don't shave me legs then?"

Gus lunged for a cushion to bash some sense into Sharma but he stopped, staring into space. She looked at him curiously. "Hello... Gus?"

The thought of bathroom smells had got him squarely, whisking the bathrug from under his feet. Shaving foam tickling the nostrils, hot steam blanking the mirror above the sink at home. Gus as a boy, sitting on the edge of the bath as dad towelled himself dry. Sodden drops of steaming air dancing around his naked torso. His firm arse, reddened and revealed as daddy gingerly pulled himself into Hawaiian print shorts, looking so tasty. Gus wanted to bite into its flesh like an apple. The kid – shivering. Father regarded him, troubled, then grinned, taking Gus in his arms. "Feel me muscles, lad."

Little hands tentatively closed around broad arms. "Nice, dad." Then, he trailed his fingers across the shoulder blade onto the chest, heart pounding. He caressed the blanket of dark hair and began to descend to the pink, semi-erect nipple that so mesmerised him. Father chortled and pushed Gus's hand away. "Steady son. That's yer mam's job."

Gus bowed his head of troubled hair, ashamed yet craving deeper. Twelve warped years of age, he was. What a jerk. He needed something to free him of his fucked-up past and enable him to fuck up his future. Something new to take his mind off this unhealthy father fixation.

"I know what I'll do," he said abruptly.

Sharma grabbed Katy Ann in a friendly, but precise neckhold, immobilising her immediately. "What's that then?" she puffed.

"You're right, you know Sharma. I shouldn't have to put up with all this bollocks."

"I'm right am I?" She didn't sound too sure.

"Yeah. No heterosexual has the right to tell me how to live my life. I should be able to fancy who I like, fuck with who I like, without having to look over my shoulder. I've played the victim long enough." To his surprise, Gus suddenly found himself on his feet. "I'll fight fire with fire. Watch me."

Sharma and Katy Ann exchanged puzzled glances. "Jesus, I'll have to ask Montgomery for more of this weed," said Sharma incredulously. Katy Ann nodded sagely.

Gus scrambled for his rucksack. "Save me some chocolate chip ice-cream, willya?" He kissed the girls and made for the door.

"Hey, where are you going?"

"Darling, the only way is up!"

Sharma pulled a face. "Oh behave!" She was going to call Gus back to check out the nude vid of her last boyfriend but he had already slammed the front door behind him.

His stockinged foot, shoe kicked off sideways, nudged the accelerator pedal that was seemingly lifelined to the cock in expansive mood beneath his chinos. Simply Red on City FM, the wide riverside avenue rushing up to meet him as the needle touched 80. Maybe it was too late for the juiciest pickings by this hour, hence the rush. Leave it too long and there were just the stragglers – the old, the ugly with more ambition than a grip on reality, scouting the headland with the characteristic animalistic glare of the starved.

True, though, that you didn't go to Otterspool to be choosy. Hang around for Prince Charming and you had a long wait ahead of you. The lookers were few and far between, and when they did rear their beautiful heads you didn't expect them to be looking for a Ken doll to add to their collection. Like most they were here to iron out the kinks in their desires that stewed unsatiated, frustrated by the judgemental gay scene which sought pretty pictures for the family album. Over here, he thought, how many times had he seen some fatty being sucked off furiously by handsome? He counted them, slowly; he had a good memory.

The mass of late night cloud cover glinted rose pink above, harbouring the city soot, nudging the temperature up a few degrees. Sweat trickled down the driver's collar; he smelt unwashed. He found it added to the mood. There was something distinctly un-English about the night, which was reassuring – with luck they would be at it like rabbits.

He caught a glimpse of bright light in the overhead mirror and switched lanes to allow a fake sports car to roar by, all puffed up fibreglass like a bloated fish. Ugly bloody thing, more money than class. The driver was proud of his German car, reeking of solid professional workmanship, well suited to his professional status as a barrister.

He normally took offence at being bullied out of his lane, but for once he understood the other driver's haste – he had been fucked by one and the same only last week, a plant manager from Birkenhead. They had crammed it in against the derelict pavilion anchoring the maze of undergrowth that Otterspool generously lent out after nightfall. They had made quite a cabaret act, more triple salcos than Torvill and Dean could ever have mustered. Speaking for himself, he got more out of the crowd participation than the miserable weeny fishing around behind.

Looming into vision at the roadside, a figure caught the driver's eye. A lone lad, balancing on the gutter edge, thumb jutting out optimistically. The sports car was already gliding past him slowly, clinging to the kerb, and he could see the kid reject him theatrically. He pressed a foot onto the brake, slowing to snail's pace. The lad spun to face him, flaring in the wide beam of his headlamps.

The skin was sugarwhite, the eyes dark and set deep, regarding him keenly through the windscreen. The hand stretched out, the thumb high, and the kid smiled, a little uncertainly. His luminosity jarred with the shadow.

The driver pulled up beside him, winding down the window. "Hiya," he smiled, keeping his composure despite his excitement. "Where are you going?"

The kid blushed. It was heavenly. "I need a lift to Otterspool." The accent was distinctly foreign, North European, something like that. The kid seemed to have stepped from a Kristen Björn porn flick into the driver's narrow world. "That's where I'm going. Get in if you like."

Worry flickered briefly in the lad's eyes as he leant through the window, his gaze darting over the car upholstery. The driver took his hands off the wheel slowly and opened his legs as wide as they would go, as much to reassure the kid as to turn him on. Nevertheless his prick was noticeably swelling in his lap. It seemed to work – the lad nodded and opened the door to sit in the passenger seat. He leant back, hands on knees. His head of curly hair faced forward, rigid. The driver scrutinised him, leaving the car engine ticking over like a contented tabby. Realising he was under observation, the kid darted a glance sideways and saw his company grinning broadly at him.

"Relax," he heard. The kid nodded again and returned the smile. "What's your name?"

"Serge. What's yours?"

"I'm Alan. Put on your seat belt and let's go, shall we darling?"

Serge nodded hurriedly and fidgeted the belt around his heaving chest into its slot. Alan put his foot flat and Serge was flung back into his seat as they roared off.

The door sprang open and Damon fell through it, nearly collapsing under the weight of the boxes he was carrying. "Jesus this is heavy! What've you got in here, Jonny?" A voice responded from the kitchen. "Mostly my 12 hole DMs, I think." Jonny's head appeared from round the door, grinning broadly. "Tape's finished."

Damon dropped the boxes and wiped a forearm across his brow. He went to the tapedeck and put the Cocteau Twin's *Treasure* into the slot. Lush, liquid melodies seeped into the room, almost invisible beneath boxes piled high to the ceiling. Despite the chaos, Damon felt ecstatic, light as air. Jonny was moving in with him. This boy, all soft grins and fine blond down across his shoulder blades, had done the unthinkable. Every hint Damon had dropped – often pretty unsubtle, causing Jonny to burst out laughing before finishing with a big kiss – every impulsive call for commitment and a serious relationship, Jonny had matched word for word. Only two weeks since they had met and yet it seemed so right. In fact, it was Jonny who had decided to move in. He had said, over dinner at a Lark Lane bistro, "I told mam about you. She was made up. She wants to meet you. Bring dad along too. I said we'd invite 'em round for dinner as soon as I'm settled in yer flat." He had grinned.

Damon had almost fallen off his chair. "Yer what? Settle in me flat?"

"Did I do the wrong thing?" asked Jonny, somewhat cockily. "I just thought–"

"Shut it!" Damon had interrupted him and clasped his hands to his head. His eyes were fuzzy and big claxon horns seemed to be going off between his temples. He waited for the hot emotion to subside and then said quietly, "When do yer wanna move yer stuff in then?"

Jonny almost vaulted over the restaurant table as he smothered Damon in kisses. The other diners had regarded them in horror, middle-aged couples in cheap scent, but they were oblivious to the spectacle they were making. They could barely keep their hands off each other. The kissing had stopped only much, much later for camomile tea and fresh towels to wipe up their pleasure.

Damon was fishing gingerly through one of the boxes when the telephone rang. Turning down the stereo, he put the receiver to his ear. "Oh, hiya Charlene."

The voice on the end of the line sounded forced, agitation ill-contained. "Damon love, have you seen Serge?"

"Not for days. Is everything alright?" Damon waited a while before he got his reply. "Everything's fine. Just fine."

Damon thought he heard someone ranting in the background.

"Have you spoken to Gus?" he asked, trying to figure out what was being said by the unknown third voice. "He spends most of his day stalking Serge."

"That one has also mysteriously disappeared," sighed Charlene.

"Well there you have it. They've finally eloped."

Damon's humour was lost on Charlene. Her voice sounded weary. "You, at least, are a good boy, aren't you Damon?"

"Well thank you very much." He was puzzled.

"How are you getting on with that lovely lad, Jonny isn't it? You'll have to introduce him to me properly some time." No offence, but Damon was intentionally steering a wide berth of Charlene and her fan club. He had no intention of letting her get her mitts on this one. "Sure I will," he reassured her.

"Good boy. Well if you hear from Serge, be sure to tell me darling? I'll leave you love birds in peace now."

"OK Charlene. Bye Charlene." Damon put down the receiver and pondered the curious phone call. He walked into the kitchen and made an appreciative noise in the back of his throat. "Babe, that food smells just too good. What is it?"

"Crusty courgette bake in a special Jonny James sauce." Jonny looked up to see Damon in hysterics. "What? What's so funny?"

"You." Jonny stood there butt naked, save for a plastic apron with Bett Lynch's face blown up on the front. As soon as Jonny saw Damon, he had stood to attention beneath its folds.

"Well Bett seems pleased to see me," said Damon ruefully. Her thick lipsticked mouth bulged incongruously.

Jonny took a peak inside his apron. He looked up with a devilish twinkle in his eye. "Well, the bake can look after itself for half an hour I reckon. And maybe you wouldn't fancy a bit of you-know-what with garlic breath and all, so…"

Damon leapt upon him, caressing his back down to his curvaceous behind. Jonny pulled at the buttons of Damon's shirt and buried his face in the chest hair that sprung up as the shirt slipped off Damon's shoulders. He bit tenderly at Damon's erect nipples, sending the boy into electric spasm. Jonny pulled the apron over his head and flung it to the floor, finally naked. Damon felt in Jonny's power. He was pushed against the tumble dryer as Jonny scrabbled at his button fly. Jonny was magnificent; taut, natural musculature across his arms and chest, furred with that same soft down, then a neat reddish garden path leading to this eager cock, cleaving the air with love and lust. Its tip glistened with liquid pearls.

"Let's finish this in the bedroom," grunted Damon. They stumbled over each other's feet to the unmade bed.

Gus sat alone in Café Tabac, supping cappuccino at closing time as the staff swept up around his feet. He was oblivious to the dirty looks they were giving him. Down his boot the blade nicked uncomfortably at his ankle. He couldn't shake the feeling that, in carrying a knife, he was asking for trouble. Still, he couldn't picture himself ever using it. He tried to imagine the sensation of sticking it in someone, the skin giving under the metal point, sinking into the soft, bloody gut. He took a double take. Like he said, he couldn't imagine ever having to use it. The knife was purely a precautionary measure.

Gus clutched tight onto the rucksack nestling in his lap. Inside: a bottle of black nail varnish; powdered amphetamines in a little silver compact; Julie Burchill's *Ambition* in paperback (he hated it but Charlene had lent it to him to read); a can of spray paint; Serge's letter, forgotten; a box of matches; a baked bean tin crammed with firecrackers.

Jonny stripped Damon naked and they swooned in their shared physicality. They fell onto the mattress, Jonny rising above Damon before descending upon the sienna prick that quivered in a bed of Greek Orthodox pubes. Moaning, Damon sank his fingertips into Jonny's hair, twisting soft curls between his fingers. Jonny swallowed Damon to the hilt and then pulled up, caressing the tip with his tongue. Damon tasted salty at the back of his throat. Down again. There was an intent in Jonny's blue eyes that Damon had never seen before. He feared it and craved it.

Jonny heaved Damon's legs around his shoulders and licked his balls, sometimes nipping at the elastic flesh. His tongue darted into the promise between Damon's cheeks. The boy squealed, pleasure rippling through his body like a summer tide. It was almost too much. "Oh Jonny…" They paused momentarily. Jonny raised his head from between Damon's legs, letting go of his straining cock. Damon felt sensations skid up and outwards from an inner coil. "Slow down," he gasped, "or I'll come."

"I want you," said Jonny thickly. "I want to fuck you."

At this an icy needle pierced Damon within. He was a virgin still. Fuck knows the desire to be screwed had assailed him in a dozen farces masquerading as love affairs. Yet he had managed to resist. Even with Jonny, making love sometimes twice, three times a day, he had maintained that distance. Was it now? Was this the moment to share the place where he hid, where no one could touch him? Was this the guy to take away that last refuge from a world that mocked his softness?

"Take me Jonny."

The boy stretched a condom over his cock and lubed up. Damon uncertainly raised his pelvis and Jonny placed a pillow beneath his arse. He sat back momentarily and admired Damon as he opened the boy's legs with his firm grip. He stroked their thick, dark hair up to Damon's arse, glistening with lube. Jonny softly whistled. "That's great Damon. Beautiful." His fingers slipped briefly into Damon, who squirmed. It was clear Jonny had done this before. Damon saw a rainbow of emotions flicker across Jonny's face.

He descended. Damon felt a strength edge into him below. It made him wince. Jonny put his fingers to Damon's lips. "Still darling. I won't hurt you. I love you." The energy penetrated further. Damon felt the colour drain from his face. Jonny managed a contorted smile to reassure him. He covered Damon's forehead with kisses as the boy's legs were pushed against his ribcage. "There…" In. "Alright?" Damon nodded in wordless intensity. Jonny began to make love to him gently at first, pulling out slowly till his cocktip rested at Damon's rosey hole, before plunging in steadily to the hilt. He moaned in tender pleasure and began to thrust faster. Damon relaxed, his tension soothed by Jonny's rhythm, swishing back and forth now, holding Damon's hairy chest for support. Damon liked that. A lot. Arched muscles subsiding, sucking greedily at Jonny's member deep in Damon's arse. A thrill, tickling Damon deep as he pulled at his cock. Jonny going slightly red, puffing. God he looks beautiful! Damon studied him, seemingly out of his tingling body as Jonny thrust harder, faster, sweat glittered on his brow like a starry sky. Jonny writhed, shuddered, as Damon worked himself with his free hand. The other clutched Jonny's arse as it rode him. Fizzy treacle began to rise within him and Jonny's eyes swirled, black outlined pools. Damon looked down to Jonny's washboard stomach taut against his legs. They both began to grunt as intense pleasure coursed through their fusing bodies. They jolted together, crying out, seeming to rise in the air. They came, Damon shooting onto Jonny's face.

Gus took out the spraycan from his rucksack. The big, white facade of the old Georgian house loomed over him, threatening to engulf his soft body. This was definitely the place. There was the window from which those lads had shouted obscenities at him and Serge.

Shards of summer luminescence scratched the night sky. The air smelt of tension and stagnant car fumes. Gus breathed in deep and pulled the lid off the aerosol can.

It popped loudly. Gus expected the street to topple onto him, bedroom lamps to flick on in uproar.

Nothing stirred.

So, after looking around, he began to spell out letters onto the facade in big, pink snakes, the aerosol hissing malevolently. As his eyes followed the arcs of his graffiti, he sped up in sensual fever. 'Born Slippy' clattered through his brain. He darted across the whole wall, covering as much of the flaking plaster as he could, standing on tiptoe to dot the 'i'. He wanted them to see this as far as Aintree.

"Fucking wild," he whispered in awe, spellbound by the complexities of this moment spelt in bright pink gas.

Curling across the doorframe and the shuttered windows, Gus's words taunted the air. "FUCK OFF HOMOPHOBIC SCUM!" In case there was any doubt as to whom he meant, the pink arrow pointing to the third floor made it very clear. Gus smiled, amazed at the exhilaration coursing through his veins. Ideas buzzed across his consciousness, crashing, interlocking, forming bigger ideas. He felt ashamed of his fear. Now things were different; he mainlined the thrill of power. He had stumbled across hate. He could tap into its inexhaustible waters just like any queerbasher that wanted to do him in. I knew my art college foundation course would amount to something, he thought wryly. He underlined his artwork with a flourish and stood back, well impressed with himself.

A noise from the end of the road brought him back to reality. He spun round to see a police car edging slowly down Percy Street, its luminescent go-faster strip flaring in the phosphorescent lamplight. Gus scrambled for his rucksack and dived behind some bins, sending a stray cat flying with a bloodcurdling howl. Gus held his breath in blind panic. The mottled tabby darted across the headlamp beams of the regulation Ford Escort as it turned into Huskisson Street. As it reached the newly desecrated wall, the police car stopped. The two occupants stared at Gus's graffiti, pointing and discussing it in agitation. One turned his head and seemed to look straight at Gus, peering out from behind the bins. His heart pounded through his head, while he kept perfectly still. His nose itched. Eventually, the police car drove on and turned into Hope Street, allowing Gus to sneeze violently.

He didn't have much time. Gus pulled out the tin of firecrackers and matches from his rucksack. Glued to the tin was a fluorescent green label with "Watch Your Backs!" written in thick black felt-tip. Gus couldn't imagine these lads having much of a sense of humour after he had finished with them. He approached the open third floor window, screwing up his left eye to judge the distance from where he stood. Some ten feet above his head, his target barely 20 centimetres high – he would only get one chance. As he lit the match, he swore at his shaking hand.

The wick of the first firecracker fizzed as it came into contact with the yellow match flame, creating a shower of blue sparks. Gus looked at the little powderkeg in his hand and momentarily considered dumping it far away over the cathedral wall. "Fuck it," he muttered and threw the tin at the open window. It soared through the air like a stricken satellite before being sucked into the darkness through the window. Gus gave a sharp intake of breath. Nothing happened.

He was about to turn tail dejected when there was an almighty snap, crackle and pop from on high, loud enough to wake the Devil. It at the very least was enough to scare the shit out of his victims, who Gus saw run screaming into the living room, afire with hot liquid sparks. He could hear the torrent of F-words and worse that spilled out of their guts. Gus clenched his fists in triumph; he was the Law. He laughed at the slapstick antics of the figures careering around their flat, bellowing hysterically at the top of their lungs. He felt the exquisite irony of the spectacle now that he had blown away their layers of machismo to reveal the pathetic wimps that cowered within.

Gus's senses slowly came back to him, enraptured as he was by the profound consequences of his actions. He realised he couldn't stand there and gloat for much longer, unless he wanted to get caught. Bedroom lamps were being flicked on; perhaps someone had already seen him there like a right idiot, pogoing insanely on the pavement. He heard a window latch being unfastened and a hundred dogs barking across town.

Gus ran down Canning Street, heart in mouth, grinning from ear to ear. Why stop here, he said to himself? Why wait for the world to catch up with its homosexuals? Why let ourselves be victimised, when there could be another, sexier coarse of action, namely fighting back? He'd show dad, make him regret ever disowning him. Gus reeled in naked aggression. But jumbled up amongst roller-coaster images of graphic vengeance, his father's face drew ever closer, taunting him, etched with loathing. Dad seemed to point accusingly at him, hurling abuse: "Faggot! Queer! You're not my son; you're not my lover! I never want to see you again!"

Gus imagined himself headbutt his dad, sending the gorgeous bigot flying in a splash of vivid red blood cells. At that, an intense, voluptuous sadness capped his rage and Gus wanted to reach down in the darkness, cradle the semi-conscious face in his hands and kiss the blood away. In his confusion, his father's face melted into Serge's. What the fuck was all this about?

Gus reached his flat and fiddled with his key in the lock. It refused obstinately to slot into place. "Come on you little shit!" Gus felt a little trickle of sweat snake down his collar. "Come *on!*" The key finally backed down and the lock gave. Once inside, he collapsed against the door. He trembled with the intensity of his train of thought, puffing like a steam train. His blood raced to his head; his heart pounded in his chest. He felt like he wanted to puke. Being right spiked him down to his soul. This was his city, splendid grime and dog-eared eccentricity. Did he want to fight it? How could he hope to take it on, its cruelty, its spite, and expect to win? He was daft to even think he could! The very people whom he identified with – the poor, the dispossessed, the rastas, the Toxteth drug barons, his own fucking family – they all despised him for his homosexuality. How could he ever win their respect? Gus shivered with a sadness that welled up in his stomach. Self-doubt ached where self-confidence had bedazzled only minutes before. He wished Serge were there, to take him in his arms, to hold him and lock the door on the real world. But he was alone. And the spectre of utter solitude waited for him deep in the darkness.

Serge's temple kept rubbing against Alan's unhooked belt, the prong jabbing his nose as he swooped on the erect cock in his face. The penis craned its moist head as though trying to peek over the dashboard. Alan fidgeted in his seat and moaned, scrabbling at his briefs which had ridden back up over his thighs and were chafing his balls. "Wait…" Alan hoisted himself up in his seat, simultaneously yanking his underpants down past his knees, and flinging behind him his mobile which had begun to insert itself up his bumhole.

Serge returned to the matter in hand – and in mouth – finding, to his surprise, that all the while he had been fondling the gearstick as though it poked out somehow from Alan's hip. Serge grunted and shifted his weight as cramp began to pinch his right leg. He sank between the seats and now had the gearstick penetrating his bellybutton. He couldn't have that. Serge raised himself forcefully and pulled a lone testicle with him. Alan's eyes snapped open, the sharp pain lassoing him. "Sorry," mumbled Serge. He returned his hand to Alan's thigh, not before noticing the tiny semen trails rolling off his chin onto the handbrake.

The belt buckle jabbed him in the eye. "Fuck!" he cursed, or some Bosnian equivalent. He rubbed furiously at his eye socket, weeping copiously over Alan's cock.

He thought Serge couldn't reach his lap and so fiddled beside him for the seat control. He disengaged sharply and the combined weight of two sent the backrest flying down, levering his groin up and ramming his cock in Serge's one good eye. Virtually blind, Serge groped around Alan's body who took the rough handling as a sign to crank up the heat a few degrees. He shoved the boy's head down enthusiastically onto his eager penis, mistaking Serge's protesting yelp for an expression of his approval.

Serge steadied himself, one hand inadvertently pawing the door mechanism and opening the window. A salty river tang billowed through the aperture, off-setting the unsavoury, hot smell of Alan's genitals. Automatically, figures loomed at the glass, peering into the car. Serge looked up and precisely at the moment he told them all to fuck off, Alan asked them "Do you want some?" smiling winsomely.

The figures retracted, one nearly losing his nose as Serge shut the automatic window. Heartily irritated, he nipped on Alan's foreskin, who consequently shook across his whole body in evident rapture. "That's good," he purred and then added with more urgency, "oh, I'm gonna come, I'm coming!"

Serge extracted the throbbing cock from his now tender throat – just in time, as a hot geyser of spunk erupted from its head and spattered the steering wheel, the windscreen, even the overhead mirror. "Oh oh oh!" gasped Alan, hanging onto the sunvisor which proceded to come off in his grasp. Serge ducked left to right to avoid the salty bullets but nevertheless came away soaked. He silently watched Alan, whose face was gurning marvellously as he writhed in his seat. In a cinematic flourish, the sweep of headlights picked out his orgasm as another car rolled up beside them. The driver, young and skinny, flicked his top heavy fringe in their direction and then moved off into the dark.

Alan pulled himself up slowly, his skin smacking as it stuck to the seat cover. "You want to come, sugar?" His voice sounded seriously diminished.

Serge shook his head. Alan looked relieved. He fixed the sunvisor back onto the roof before retrieving his underwear from around his feet. His cock had shrunk to nothingness, Serge noticed maliciously.

When Alan had finished buttoning his chinos at his waistline, he gave Serge a brisk, business-like smile. "So, I'll be taking you home then?"

The boy stiffened. Home. He didn't for one minute imagine he would be too welcome there after tonight. Charlene would be after his blood. Serge peered through the windscreen at the gloom outside and shivered. "No, I will stay here a bit more," he said.

Alan regarded him curiously and then began to fish around in his trouser pocket. He unearthed a twenty pound note and pressed it into Serge's palm. The boy looked wounded. "I'm not rent," he hissed, trying to return the money to Alan.

"I know. But take it as a compliment. You sucked me off like a pro. You should think about it – it always helps to pay the bills. Nothing wrong with that. Besides, I at least owe you the taxi fare back."

Serge studied the note in his hand. The Queen smiled back at him malevolently, tempting him with all manner of evils. "Thanks." He pocketed the money. "Well, see you then."

Alan buckled his seatbelt and switched on the radio. Simply Red on City FM. "I hope so." Serge opened his door and climbed out, feeling the late, late chill wrap itself around his shoulders. Alan's German car navigated past him and away, dousing him in an acrid cloud of exhaust fumes.

Jonny collapsed onto Damon, spent. They lay there panting, bodies glistening with a thin film of sweat. This time they had fucked slowly, leisurely; trying different positions, discovering intimate symbiosis. Gone was the desperate urgency of their first coupling; instead they had wallowed in each other, nerves tingling, sensitive to the merest shift in rhythm and pressure. They had controlled their orgasms, so often teetering on the brink – Damon bit so hard on his bottom lip he drew blood – but always pulling back in search of heaven. Then it became impossible to tame their desire any longer; Jonny thrashed on top of Damon, lost in orgasmic trance. They had near spontaneously combusted as spunk ripped out of their steel-reinforced cocks. Then Jonny collapsed onto Damon, spent.

A soft breeze played upon them from the open bedroom window. The stillness hummed across their bodies.

Damon cast an eye on the clock radio. It blinked from 03:47 to 03:48. Jesus, had they really been at it *that* long? He looked at Jonny, who seemed to be succumbing to deep sleep, his breath regularising and serene. Jonny's eyelashes shimmered as the last traces of energy coiled across his spent body. Damon felt faintly ridiculous, his legs wrapped around Jonny's neck. He cleared his throat sheepishly. An eye flicked open above him and lingering on Damon's flushed cheeks.

"Fuck! The dinner!" Jonny leapt up and out of Damon as the smell of burning garlic wafted in from the kitchen. A soggy condom did a mid-air somersault and Damon watched an arse jig out of the bedroom. The condom landed on his shoulder. Vanilla flavour. Damon shut his eyes and a smile escaped onto his face.

"Shit," said Jonny, walking back into the bedroom whilst rubbing his groin with a clean towel. "Dinner's ruined, darling."

"That's OK," said Damon. "I've kind of lost my appetite. Come back to bed." Jonny grinned and tweaked his still semi-erect cock. "Ready for Round Three, are we?"

"I had a deathwish last year, Buck Rogers. Save it for the morning." He cradled Jonny in his arms, who licked his soft, pink nipple like a puppy. "I just want you to know how much I love you," continued Damon, stroking Jonny's curly hair. "People have always made fun of me 'cos I'm pretty soft. And I hurt real easy – I go a bit weird sometimes. But that was the Just Seventeener in me, babe. You make me feel the opposite Jonny — kind of strong. With you I can tell the world where to get off. This time it's for real."

Jonny spoke somewhat drowsily. "I hope you're not going all butch on me." His head sank into his chest as the head massage he received from Damon began to take effect.

Damon realised he sounded a bit melodramatic. "Butch, me? I'm more bitch than butch, lover boy." He smirked and looked down at Jonny, who had already closed his eyes and was beginning to snore lightly. Damon lowered him onto the pillow and admired his handsome face. A contented smile played on Jonny's ruby lips.

Damon felt like the fuck of the century. He might not be able to sit down for a week but it was worth it for the helter skelter high. He felt whole, as if the last part in the puzzle had been fitted after being lost all these years down the back of the sofa. It seemed that life's trial and error had been building up to this moment of glory. No more mid rum and coke crisis. No more crackpot therapies. Just him and Jonny, rewriting the rule book.

Damon yawned. Best get some shut-eye. Tomorrow was to be a big day of unashamed domesticity. It seemed to him as remarkable as shooting stars and sunbursts.

Damon was fluffing up his pillow when there was an earth-shattering racket from outside. It sounded for all the world like a dozen firecrackers going off. Jonny stirred and groaned. "What the fuck was that?"

"Don't know babe." Damon rose and went to the window. From over the rooftops he could see flashes of light crackle somewhere in Huskisson Street. Damon frowned. "Can't see for sure. Maybe an electrical fire in a house or something."

Jonny raised his head from the pillow. "Do you think they might need help?"

"Let's just see. It already seems to have stopped." Damon did a double-check as he saw a familiar figure dart down an alleyway. Didn't that look like Gus? What was he doing out at this time of night? Nah — can't have been him. Damon climbed back into bed and ran his fingers down to Jonny's rock hard crotch.

"I think it's alright." He cupped his lover's chin in his hand and kissed him full on the lips. "Now, what about Round Three?

Serge brushed imaginary cobwebs off his face and stepped forward slowly, identifying a hazy group of figures circling to one side. They prowled around each other as if in the preliminary to an all-male square dance. It was the usual cross section of faces, hell-bent on copulation: the perennial closet middle-aged family types in dire need of cock; the old and infirm hobbling uncertainly, in dire need of cock; the scene queens gone stale, in dire need of cock. And Serge? What was he doing here?

One or two looked promising, opening up the flank to let him silently into their midst. Serge took up the invitation, hoping they couldn't tell he was scared silly. Think of it as therapy, he reminded himself. Yet each time he returned here, he laid himself wide open. He wondered if some deeply ingrained gluttony for punishment made him one of the regulars at Otterpool.

One fella, thirty-odd, not bad looking actually, veered off up a bracken path. Serge watched him go; he was limping, always dragging his left foot behind him. The man turned his head and stared fixedly at Serge, before continuing. The boy felt heat rising to his cheeks. He nodded and began to follow the man up a rise into a clump of trees, always remaining a few steps behind. The man quickened his pace suddenly and was swallowed up by the gloom, not even looking back once. Alarmed, Serge giant-stepped the last few yards and vaulting a patch of higher ground, emerged into a secluded clump of vegetation. He saw he was perfectly hidden from the path just a couple of feet away. He stopped and looked around. The air whispered sweet nothings, licking at the dry summer leaves.

The man regarded him from one corner, etched in silhouette. The eyes glinted. He stepped forward briskly and gripped Serge's shoulders. The boy didn't resist. He raised his chin to meet the man's slippery mouth, who immediately lodged his tongue deep down Serge's throat. The man pulled back, licking his lips. "I can taste – spunk." Serge nodded and shrugged. The man grinned. "You dirty little bugger." He clamped his mouth again to Serge's, pulling at the lad's waist, lifting his T-shirt and running rings around his chest. His nipples smarted as fingers brushed close. Serge, over-excited, clawed at the man's zipper and plunged his hand down his trousers, squeezing hard on the stiff cock that met his grasp. The fella took a sharp intake of breath, pulling back a second. "Watch it…" he hissed in a broad Scouse twang.

Serge nodded hurriedly but insisted, flicking the man's belt open and roughly yanking his trousers to his knees. He saw off-white Y-fronts and wasted no time in bypassing those too. The man's dick bounded like a bungee jumper. "Fucking Christ," Serge heard, "you're keen. Turn around then."

Dumbly, Serge did as he was told. His trousers and Calvins were likewise dispensed with and he felt a silken breeze tickle his now prostrate arse. He breathed heavily, urgently, screwing his eyes tight shut. Warning bells began to ring in his head as he waited for something to happen. The fella was rubbing his cock along Serge's crack, gasping each time his penis hit a right-angle against the firm flesh. Serge's panic welled at each simulated thrust, till it became near unbearable. He was a stupid bastard, that was what he was. A hot flush of codified memories transfixed him, sparked by his sudden vulnerability. His arse ached with the spell. One after the other, so many pricks doing him, him dripping with spit and cum, his screams drowned by their excited whoops and shrieks, taunting him to the tune of the Serbian national anthem. Serge shook. Get out of there. Too late. He felt the man's soft breath at his arse, pulling his cheeks apart slowly. "Nice, very nice," the man whistled, before burying his face in Serge's hole. He felt a tongue lash him hot inside; it stabbed him like a knife. He jolted. His dick found his hand and he began to pull himself off sharpish. The guy behind sank ever deeper into his warm insides, making all sorts of smacking noises with his chops.

Serge began to spasm, his spine no longer able to hold himself up. He tipped forward, only kept upright by the incredible suction on his arsehole. The man was wanking himself too, and pearly pinballs of semen already shimmied in the air, spat from his jerking penis. Serge swished left to right and ejaculated in the air before him, almost snapping the man's tongue off inside his rectum. He sprung backwards, surprised at the strength of Serge's bum muscles. His cock bounced about, shooting liquid cotton everywhere. His face was still scrunched up, glistening ruddily with spit.

Serge sank to his knees. He felt appalled, wretched.

"Good eh?" said the man, patting Serge on the head as he pulled himself to his feet, lifting his trousers with him in one deft movement. "Tasty," he added, as though describing lunch, "all sorts of interesting sensations in there. Thanks a lot." Having straightened himself out, the man slipped through the undergrowth without another word, leaving Serge hunched over on the ground.

Through the cover of vegetation, he could see the flicker of motion near and far, hear the rustle of wildlife and wilder, the occasional human cry piercing the air. Serge's arse felt soaking, unpleasant. He pulled a tissue from his pocket and wiped diffidently at his cock.

He considered what he should do now. Serge rubbed his arm brusquely, feeling chilly. Looking around him, he saw that if he pulled away some undergrowth beyond the small clearing, he could probably crash undisturbed for a couple of hours. He felt exhausted. He floated. He needed rest. He began to pull at the creepers vigorously, pulling them up into a makeshift bed.

5

SHARMA SAT AT HER DRESSING TABLE, applying her make-up in the mirror. She wore kohl across the eyes to accentuate the ivory of her steady gaze, its dusky trail sinking into her sienna complexion. She was crayoning her lips bordeaux in precise strokes. Her thick, dark hair was up, tied in a black flower. She smelt of Donna Karan, bought New Year in downtown New York. She played PJ Harvey on the stereo, her half-empty wine glass rattling beat by beat near her pile of cosmetics.

She checked her watch and cursed the hour. He would be here any minute now and she wasn't even dressed yet. Her lace armour of bodice and suspender intricacy cut deep into her flesh, pushing her breasts to the outer limits and cutting her respiration. She didn't make this effort for everyone, the ritualistic embalming of her body to entrance the opposite sex, but this was a special dinner date. Katy Ann was staying at friends in Waversley, so the house was spared her peculiar, intense energy, allowing Sharma to rise to the occasion. Her daughter wouldn't approve, she knew. She sat back and studied her immaculate reflection.

Satisfied with her face paint, she pulled the little black velvet dress from its hanger and stepped into its loops. It clung to her curves like a spiderweb. The doorbell rang as she adjusted her chest accordingly. Emitting a little squeak of frustration, she scrambled for her black stilettos amongst the shoes that littered the bedroom carpet. Turning to leave, she smoothed her silhouette in the full-length mirror encrusted with *X-Files* cut-ups and tabloid pics of David Duchovny in an early career soft porn venture. She tugged at her fringe, allowing a kiss-curl to tumble coquettishly onto her forehead. Not bad at all. Guzzling the contents of her wine glass, she hurtled downstairs to the front door, behind which outside a solitary figure wavered.

Sharma took a deep breath and opened the door. She challenged her visitor with a dazzling smile.

"Hiya gorgeous."

"Hiya Sharma. Thanks for the dinner invitation." Serge produced a raggedy bunch of flowers from behind his back. "For you."

Sharma took them, snorting loudly on their fragrance. "You're a sweetheart. But you really shouldn't go around raiding my neighbours' window boxes on my behalf."

Serge grinned sheepishly and stepped into the passageway. "Wipe yer feet." Sharma looked him up and down curiously, from the mud on his boots to the grass clinging to his shirt. "Where have you been? You look like you've been dragged through a hedge backwards." She sniffed. "And you smell worse."

Serge coloured. "I didn't come home last night. I've runned away."

Sharma stared at him boggle-eyed for a moment before regaining her composure. "Right. In you come then." She took Serge's hand and led him to the living room. In one corner was a small table covered with a white cloth, two places set and candles burning, letting off a slightly acrid odour.

Serge took in the soft-lit scenario. "This is very… cosy."

"Thankyou. Sit." Sharma motioned towards the sofa. "I wanted this to be special. God knows I've waited a long time to get you all to myself. You're a difficult boy to pin down."

Serge hesitated as he sank into the sofa. "I always am busy. You know, English lessons at nights and then Charlene got me work for a few days on a building site in Birkenhead." Sharma's scent wafted under his nose. He sniffed. "But such a big effort you have made for me. Why?"

"Because, gorgeous." Sharma sat beside him, making serious eye contact. Serge wriggled uncomfortably. "What's going on?" she asked.

Serge took a deep breath. "You'll find out soon, I bet. Charlene will send out the dogs to catch me if she doesn't already."

Sharma frowned. "You haven't got on the wrong side of her, have you?" She shifted closer on the sofa, resting a hand on Serge's shoulder.

"I don't care," said Serge punkily. "I'm not scared of her, or her old drag queens."

"Oooh darling, how thoroughly male you are," Sharma cooed, looking at him with a Bordeaux smile playing on her lips. "I hope for your sake you're right. I'd hate to think what they'd do to you if they got their hands on you." Her flippancy was grimly underlined. "A pack of rabid trannies – they'd rip you to shreds with a couple of put downs and then finish you off with their false nails."

"Yeah well, they won't get a chance with me." Serge flicked at an imaginary fluff ball on his trousers. "You, Sharma, you never really liked Charlene did you?" he asked. "Tell me what she did to wind you up."

Sharma considered. Serge looked wounded, forlorn. She understood his hurt; whatever had happened between him and Charlene, a bust-up with your parent (even a surrogate, gender-bending one) could be traumatic. To a point, Serge owed her everything.

"I never had anything against Charlene," said Sharma cautiously. "Just for the sake of Katy Ann I've always kept a fair distance." She twirled a finger softly through Serge's curls. "I've seen the way she plays off you boys against each other and I don't like it. Look at you now, having to hide out like a hit and run."

Serge nodded slowly. "Why do you think she does that?"

"I think…" Sharma felt an intense yearning to bury the boy's head in her breast. She hurriedly scribbled out the image mentally. "I think she cares a lot for all of you but she can't appear to be too soft." Sharma watched Serge falter at her every word. "Let's change the subject, eh?" she said briskly. "Have you had anything to eat?"

"Not since yesterday. I'm very starving."

"OK. We'll soon rectify that. Now why don't you go and take a shower?" Sharma wrinkled her nose. "What have you been up to?"

Serge sniffed his armpits gingerly. "Do I smell that bad?"

"Like a lesbian from Emmerdale." Sharma shook her head. "I really don't want to know where you ended up last night."

Serge slowly let a mischievous grin surface on his face; it was like sun peeking from behind rainclouds.

"Actually I did have a fat cock for dinner last night."

Sharma tutted and slapped Serge hard on his behind. It made a satisfying smacking sound. Sharma felt her palm tingle in gratification. "No pudding for you then. Honestly," she grumbled, "why is all the sex being had by everyone but me?" She hustled Serge towards the door. "You'll find a clean towel on the rail," she yelled, as she watched his cute arse wiggle down the passageway in the direction of the bathroom.

Sharma was standing over a pot in the kitchen when she heard the shower being switched off, followed by the dull thump of Serge's feet clambering out onto the fleecy bathrug. She turned down the gas to simmer and crept along to the bathroom door. Serge was puffing and panting as he rubbed himself vigorously with the towel.

Sharma hesitated and rapped lightly on the door. She heard Serge pause and then answer slowly. "Uh huh?"

"You alright, love?"

"Fine."

Sharma placed both hands outstretched on the door panelling and rested her head slowly inbetween. Serge was breathing soft, a regular intake of humid air. "Why don't you wear my bathrobe love, rather than those dirty old clothes? I'll arrange getting some of your gladrags to you in the meantime."

There was a pause again before Serge answered. "Oh I don't know…"

"Oh, go on!" exclaimed Sharma, trying to sound as natural as possible. "Don't be a ninny. It's behind my bedroom door, first on your left. Oh, and use whatever smellies you like."

"Thank you."

Sharma retreated, sensing a thrill-worm wriggle in the pit of her stomach. Scurrying round the corner, she pressed herself against a wall and listened as Serge hesitantly opened the bathroom door. He emerged into the hallway and padded down as far as the bedroom, feet soft mushing on the shag pile. Sharma cursed the scene of cosmetic mayhem that was her inner sanctum, but it was too late now. She heard Serge slip round the door and poking her head out from her hiding place, she caught a glimpse of a snow-white posterior.

Sharma tiptoed over to her bedroom. The door rocked as her robe slipped off its hook around Serge's shoulders. Sharma braced herself and swung the door wide open. Serge stood there, regarding her in alarm, hurriedly trying to tie the gown at his waist. Sharma caught a photo flash of loins, a heavy cock lying coy in a bed of pubic vegetation. The image would remain with her to her dying day.

"Serge!" Sharma affected mock surprise. "I thought you were still in the bathroom." She tried to gloss over his discomfort. "I was just going to tidy my bedroom a bit. Don't worry love. Once you've seen one you've seen them all. Nothing to be ashamed of there."

Serge frantically tied a double knot at his waist. "Finished now," he said awkwardly.

"Right love. Hurry up and come through. Dinner's nearly ready." She paused to assess Serge's attire. "Don't look too bad on you."

Serge waved his arms vaguely. "Sleeves too short." His thick arms poked out too far from the holes.

"I won't tell if you won't. Don't be long." Sharma flashed Serge a disarming smile and exited sharpish. As she emerged into the kitchen, she couldn't help the triumphant exhilaration etched on her face.

The bonfire had been visible for miles around, over the haggard city roofs and beyond, pulsing like a bleeding heart in the Toxteth cavity. As Gus reached the split, punctured housing state off North Hill, he noticed the curious chunk missing from its pebble dash flank and expected to witness a Tyrannosaurus loping off down to the Mersey with a few Scousers in its jaw. A blue, Tory rosette pinned to its scaly hide would not have looked out of place. But no, this was simply the result of inner city wear and tear – the tramping of bovver boots, the intensity of rush hour drug traffic. It was so degradingly familiar it was almost quaint, fit for a picture postcard.

The fire flowered into view, holding court in the middle of bracken wasteland, humping the burnt-out shell of a stricken Ford Capri. The flames whooshed up, clinging onto air currents, gorging on the evening's sullen spell and the tang of dry gasoline. Around its billowing edge, a crowd of impassive onlookers confronted the spectacle with the mute resignation of the chronically numb. A pack of screeching, whooping kids livened things up, hurling projectiles into the orange barbecue. The fireball roared its approval. Somewhere nearby, a doberman barked incessantly, frustrated within the shoe-cupboard confines of an empty flat, his owner off down the local. Police sirens added to the wall of sound, but kept their distance, busy enough elsewhere on the city battleground.

Gus joined the massing throng, wishing to feel part of something, even neighbourhood disintegration. He was desperate for human contact; he had risen that morning nauseous with the sinking feeling that he had FUCKED UP in big capital letters. He had taken on the day by trying to fool himself into believing it was just like any other, but wandering around town his crime seemed stamped onto his forehead. Down Bold Street his ears burned with the nagging suspicion that housewives discussed him in his wake – he would turn and they flicked back to the fruit'n'veg.

Gus sidled up to a shell-suited family clutching each other tight as the Ford Capri sank deeper into its grave, tyres popping in a shower of sparks. He was spellbound by their intimate appreciation of the sideshow; mam, dad and the kiddies sharing shrill laughs. Gus envied their queasy, slightly rank closeness. He speculated that his own family was cut from the same coarse cloth – now he had the emotional distance to reflect on the past and be selective, just the prime-time memories for playback, please. His folks wouldn't have been out of place here, revelling in the pyrotechnics, shouting over each other in the scramble to be the loudest and the lariest. He saw the one babby extending a pinkie furtively up his nostril, fishing around for scraps. Dad witnessed this too; Gus winced at the whack the kid got, clean across his skull. The little, dishevelled boy registered surprise before realising that, if he had any sense, he had better switch on the waterworks. Face beetroot, he opened his mouth wide and let out an almighty howl. Mam scooped him up into her arms and back-chatted her hubby with a frighteningly colourful vocabulary, him standing there taking the barrage of abuse.

"Hey mate, got a ciggy?" Gus looked down to see a pale, gingery boy in baggy Moschino sneering up at him. Gus shook his head hurriedly; the kid looked about ten years old. Gus stepped back, the lad sniggering, "Poof," before running off to rejoin his gang dancing around the fire. Chastened, Gus decided it was time to make a get-away. He felt like he needed some speed to perk himself up. And some cock, unsurprisingly. He looked back to the flames listlessly; the Capri smouldered, glowing dull vermilion against the rapidly darkening sky. In the forbidding porridge of decrepit council estates, it pulsed with a stark, transitory beauty. The crowd began to disperse, quietened by the car's swansong.

A hand pulled roughly at Gus's shoulder. He looked behind him to see a hulking figure blocking his path. Despite the twilight, the bloke's face was familiar.

"Winny?" He was so called because, tall and wide, he bore an imposing resemblance to Oprah before she could fit into a size 12. "You're to come with me, Gus." His voice was a foghorn, but still gave away his Jamaican roots. He gripped Gus tighter with his paw and nearly lifted him off his feet as he steered him towards the Carmen Ghia parked in a bus shelter that was seemingly chainsawed in half.

Gus struggled in vain to free himself from Winny's grip. As they approached the vehicle, the rear door swung open and he was bundled in.

"Look at you! You resemble a frigging bog brush. Is that what's fashionable these days?" Gus composed himself and peered in the dim light at the speaker who regarded him from the front passenger seat. The face was wrapped in bandages, shades obscuring the eyeholes and a spliff protruding from the slit for a mouth. A Pekinese growled at him, muzzled, from the figure's lap.

"Madame Lafayette?" he faltered. "You don't look too good yourself."

Next to him, a thin as a rake Edie Sedgwick clone dug sharp fingernails into his forearm. "Watch your mouth!" Her make-up glowed like ectoplasm.

Madame Lafayette raised a hand in reconciliation. "Leave the boy, Miss Golightly," she sighed. "He does have a point after all. Here, have some of this." She passed the joint to Gus and pulled at a few wisps of hair dancing over her brow, fixing them back into her hairpiece. "Now, down to business. You've been a busy boy, haven't you Gus?"

He sank into the car upholstery, savouring the fire slipping down his throat. "Meaning…?"

Miss Golightly piped up. "Meaning you've been making a fucking mockery of our operation and leaving us to clear up the mess."

Madame Lafayette 'tsked' at her in irritation and motioned for quiet.

"You've lost me," said Gus.

"I don't think so," corrected Madame Lafayette. "Just promise me from now on you won't go wandering around Toxteth like Bo Peep who's lost her sheep, for Chrissakes. You do realise you have them all looking for you, and if they catch you they'll have your knackers for supper?"

"Not if I get there first," muttered Miss Golightly under her breath. Gus glowered mutely at her.

Madame Lafayette swivelled her swathed head to face the front. "I told Charlene you lads were hopeless. But she's too busy thinking with her cunt to notice."

She motioned for Winny to drive off.

Sharma walked into the lounge, laden with plates and cutlery. As she laid the table, Serge sat upright and awkward on the sofa. He held the hem of the bathrobe to his knees as it threatened to ride up and reveal his privates. Sharma thought he curiously aped the pose of a tight-skirted office secretary in a *Carry On* farce. "What'll yer listen to?" She bent down, scrabbling amongst the scattered CDs by the hi-fi.

"Whatever."

"Whatever. That's a big help." She inserted a disc and pressed play, pulling herself to her feet. "I hope this tickles your fancy." Toni Braxton's *Secrets* billowed across the room. "Mmmm…" Sharma rocked her hips to the beat. "Did you know this song's about her fingering herself while thinking about her bloke? The hussy!"

Serge clutched his knees in mock-horror. "I'm not sure I'm hungry any more."

Sharma giggled and dived onto the sofa. The upholstery flexed, nearly tipping Serge into her lap. She raised an arm and Serge flinched involuntarily. "Don't worry, I've washed me hands." Sharma trailed a nail across the boy's shoulder and regarded him brazenly. "Well, since when did you go all sweet and innocent?"

"Since when you started talking about women's bits." Serge wriggled uncomfortably as Sharma draped herself over his lap. "No talking dirty before dinner."

Sharma smiled. Serge smelt of her Ananya shower gel and it was all rather erotic. "I like a man with a healthy appetite. What can I get you to drink while I check on the oven?"

"A beer is fine."

Sharma tottered off to the kitchen on her precarious heels. Serge's eyes bulged at the voluptuous display of flesh and he felt distinctly vulnerable. He knew this Sharma from long nights chaperoning her in dreadful straight clubs. He shuddered at the thought that she was bored with straight men and was looking for a challenge.

Sharma bustled back into the lounge with a dish of Japanese pretzels and a Sol. "One beer – and something for you to nibble on." She plunged onto the couch beside Serge and batted her eyelids demurely, staring intently into Serge's peepers. He cleared his throat. "Where's Katy Ann tonight?"

"She's staying at a mate's house. It's just you and me and a crateful of Bulgarian Beaujolais."

Serge fought the sinking feeling lodged in the pit of his stomach "Why me – when you could be on your back with Stan Collymore, for example?"

Sharma laughed and shook her head. "Nah – he was all mouth and no trousers." She placed her tiny hand in Serge's. "It's always the same with footballers. All looks pretty smashing at kick-off, by the final whistle he's rushing off to shower with the boys."

"What I'd do to be a bar of soap…" Serge threw back his head and stretched languorously.

Sharma jabbed a finger in his ribs. "Cheeky! Of course, in your case it's quantity, not quality, you're interested in. It's your age. Believe me, I've been there and back and I can't wait to move on to pastures new." Sharma eyeballed Serge with a mysterious glint in her eye. "Serge, have you ever – been with a woman before?"

He took a deep swig on his beer. "Why do you want to know?" he asked cautiously. The alcohol fizzed on his tongue like pepper.

"Indulge me."

Serge cast his mind back, frowning. "Do you mean – having sex?"

Sharma rubbed her hands together with barely suppressed glee. "Do I ever! Have you?!"

"I might have." Serge suddenly felt on the defensive.

"And…?"

"Well, I did my best, but I prefer to having something to hold onto." He shrugged. "They seemed happy, I think. City girls, you know, picking up lonely army boys from the hills. I didn't know better and they paid well."

Sharma clasped a hand to her forehead. "Ger'away! They paid you?! Quick, I'll go and get me purse."

Serge interjected hurriedly, "I don't do tricks any more."

Sharma looked crestfallen. "Shame. I've got quite a few mates who'd happily fork out for a bit of Bosnian cock. It could have been a nice little earner."

Serge bristled. "I know more than to use my penis, OK!"

"I bet you can love. Do tell."

Serge groaned. "Why does no one believe me?" Sharma snickered to herself for managing to make a bloke squirm – she enjoyed giving fellas a taste of their own medicine – but felt enough pity for Serge to call it quits.

"Course I do, Serge. So – what are yer going to do? I'm all ears." She leaned forward, listening intently.

The boy thought for a moment. "I don't want to go back to Charlene's. I really don't. She can find someone else to do the dirty work."

Sharma looked confused. "What are you carping on about?"

"Sssh!" Serge glanced over his shoulder.

"I've checked the place for bugs," said Sharma impatiently. "You don't have to whisper."

"I hear Charlene on the telephone sometimes. She's trying to take over Dale Street and the village from the gangs – you know, control the drugs, the rent, the bars. She and her tranny army – they're dangerous, man. Sharma! Don't laugh! I'm serious!"

"I'm sorry," she cackled. "You're asking me to believe Liverpool gangland is quaking in its boots over a bunch of Dolly Parton lookalikes?"

"Think about it. You know Charlene's past. She has contacts. She's could do it. She's confident enough now to go for big money. That's why all this queerbashing is happening. The gangs know Charlene's plans and a lot of people don't like it. Can you imagine the mafia will take orders from a drag queen?"

Sharma's eyes widened as certain things began to fall into place. "Gus told me what happened to you two the other night, being hassled and all."

"Gus?" Serge's face screwed up. "Oh him." He stifled a yawn.

Sharma looked at him disparagingly.

"What?" protested Serge.

"Well, what's going on with you and Gus?"

"Not much."

"Bollocks!"

"We tried and it just doesn't work. End of story."

Sharma snorted derisively. "Just because you couldn't arrange a decent hard-on between the pair of you in one abortive shag attempt? Something tells me you mean more to each other than a quickie."

"He tell you that?"

"Well, what is it about you two that refuses to budge, anyway?"

Serge shrugged his shoulders. "I don't know." He took a deep breath. "Maybe I'm tired of fighting these days. He's a bloody head case." Serge sighed. "Cute though."

"He's had some problems – drugs, bad experiences with blokes and all that," admitted Sharma. "All he needs is you to be straight with him. God, I'm asking the wrong fella to be straight. Another beer?"

Serge looked uncertain. "I'm a slut when I get pissed…"

Sharma looked hard at Serge. "Oh go on. I should be so lucky." With that she catwalked through to the kitchen and re-emerged, beer in hand. "You can stay here you know, Serge – until you sort yourself out. Katy Ann would be made up."

"Me? Stay here?" Serge mulled it over: home cooked meals; an endless stream of gorgeous homophobes passing by his door; babysitting a precocious brat while Sharma went out on the pull…

Serge blinked. He chose to fob off the invitation for now. "Katy Ann? How is she?"

"My pride and joy," beamed Sharma, taking the bait. "She's been getting a petition together among her classmates against the heterosexual bias in school textbooks."

Serge guffawed. "I think it's difficult to be her mother, no?"

"As far as she is concerned, I'm a victim of the white, male-dominated status quo. It's brilliant. I can fuck up spectacularly and she forgives me for everything."

"Lucky you," said Serge drily.

"Serge love, I am not the sort to moan of being a victim blah blah blah, but even I admit it's not easy, this single mum lark. I have me parents on me back to tie the knot with Katy Ann's biological father for a start. To tell yer the truth, I'm not even sure who the father was. I had three blokes on the go at the time."

Serge nearly choked on his beer. "And you tell me you need to get out more?" he exclaimed incredulously.

"Thank God Katy Ann didn't turn out like any of those three losers," continued Sharma, snagged on a train of thought. "Then there's my weasel of a brother who can do no wrong, according to my parents. Right spoilt little brat. If only they knew his allowance goes towards sustaining his cocaine addiction. I give him six months before he's found gunned down on Princes Avenue. I do what's best for me and for Katy Ann in the circumstances, and I'm a right slapper in their eyes."

Sharma came and sat down by Serge, resting her hand lightly on his bare kneecap. Slowly she began to slip her fingers under the bathrobe. "You know," she said mischievously, "I even considered presenting you to me parents as my betrothed."

Serge gaped at Sharma without a word.

"Think about it from your point of view. You can't stay here for much longer without some sort of legal status. Then it would help get me parents off me back. I was lucky not to get shipped off to marry some spotty cousin from Islamabad."

Serge shook his head. "It won't work. I like boys and their toys."

Sharma waved a hand dismissively. "The logistics we'll figure out when we get there. I've already been told I fuck like a fella. One said after a night with me he felt like he'd been raped."

Serge bent down to Sharma's level and kissed her drunkenly on the lips without a second's hesitation. "You, Sharma, are mad too, I think."

She licked her lips hungrily. "Well, I'll leave the offer open. I'd be happy to have you for a husband. There's a shortage of good men around here. The fact that you are an aberration in the eyes of the Lord can be overlooked just this once."

Serge chuckled, downing the dregs of his wine glass. "Alright Sharma, I'll stay tonight at least. But hands on the table always. This relationship is going is completely plutonic." He grabbed her hand, crawling ever closer to the cock between his thighs, and placed it back on her lap.

"Party pooper," scowled Sharma. She stood and her boobs bounced accordingly in her little black dress. "God, I'm a babe," she announced. "That's platonic actually, my love." She smiled fondly at Serge as he sat trussed up in her bathrobe. "Why don't you give Gus a ring while I serve dinner? Get the ball rolling?"

Serge shook his head. "No way. You must be mad." On cue the telephone squawked from amongst the CDs. "Well, what timing," remarked Sharma. "I take it you're not here?" Serge shook his head. "I thought so."

As Sharma attended to the telephone, Serge's attention drifted to her bookshelf: Valerie Solanis's *S.C.U.M. Manifesto;* Kathy Acker; *Orlando; A Cosmo Reader.* Sharma was certainly wise to the times. He pulled out a well-thumbed biography of Madonna circa *True Blue,* all trash graphics and big print. He skimmed the sycophantic text impatiently. Though his back was turned, he sensed Sharma standing behind him, her arms reaching out to snake around his waist. He spun round.

Sharma's arms dropped to her side. "Speak of the Devil. That was Gus on the phone. Sounded pretty frantic, actually."

Serge rolled his eyes. "Drama queen, you see? What's his problem?"

"He wouldn't say. He wants us all to get together tomorrow evening, though Charlene's only back from hosting the tranny symposium in Oslo next week."

"That's good."

"Gus said it was she who suggested this meeting."

Serge frowned. "Maybe it's a trap?"

"I shouldn't think so," scoffed Sharma. "This is dull as dishwater Merseyside. You watch too much telly."

She cocked her head and smiled. "Maybe it's just the Grand Unveiling of his pierced peeny."

Serge looked sideways at Sharma. "Peeny...?" he asked uncertainly.

She rolled her eyes. "Penis love. Penis."

6

Jonny polished off the oily egg scraps clinging to his plate, aware, all the while, of the labourer-type fella in dungarees scrutinising him from the window seat, flecked with paint down to his Caterpillar boots. He held up today's *Sun* over which he regarded Jonny; his eyes were brown and heavy lashed, enough to justify a quicky if Jonny had been that way inclined. As it was he was distracted by the front-page mug shot of Robbie Williams, recently relieved of his duties in Take That. Robbie, too, glared over his beer belly at Jonny with heavy-bagged eyes. The mighty – how they fall, thought Jonny distractedly. The headline screamed insults at the ex-boy wonder, slating his drunken antics. Jonny recalled he had always kept a photo cutout of Take That in his school pencil case, culled furtively from the pages of *Mizz* when his classmates weren't looking. It was an early publicity shot, from the time when the homo angle was emphasised in the scramble for a larger public. The boys cuddled topless in pre-piercing innocence, Robbie anchored to Mark, nipples almost touching, Robbie's sprouting hair, and Mark's smooth and hairless. It certainly had been enough to energise a fledgling Jonny – the tummy butterflies didn't lie. The girls huddled around the latest *Just 17* exposé, adrenalised into puppy love, not seeing how queer the set-up really was. Jonny grimaced now at the flabby, hit-less monster floundering in the detritus of his illustrious career; those girls were probably already pushing prams. Take that indeed, he thought wryly.

The labourer had a bloody sliver of Ketchup dripping down his chin. Jonny, smiling measuredly, pointed at his own chin to alert the fella to the fact. The man responded by licking away the E number trail with his tongue, all the while eyeballing Jonny. One supposed this was all the invitation he needed; he looked away hurriedly.

He waved at Jackie who, fag in mouth, was busy dropping ash over the clean tables. She nodded brightly and came over, pulling her notepad and pencil from her apron. "You off then?" Her voice scratched the smoky air.

"Yup."

"That's three pound twenty, Jonny love." As he fished around for pennies, Jackie struck up conversation. "So how's life on the right side of the tracks?"

Jonny grinned. "So you do miss me then, do you Jackie?"

She scratched at her ribs absent-mindedly with her pencil. "Miss yer? Not just me babe. Half the women round here, their whoopsies have shrivelled up since you buggered off." She noted the fifty pence tip he pressed into her palm. "Ta love, come again."

Jonny stood and sauntered jauntily out the caff into the dusty street. The parked cars shimmered in the early afternoon heat, the traffic burble tickling his ears. Jonny checked his watch and began to head off, when he detected a flurry of movement behind him. He turned.

"Jonny! Where do yer think yer goin'?" The labourer type raced up to him. He was actually smaller than Jonny had imagined, but built like a Bantam cock. "How'd you know me name?" Jonny frowned.

"I heard that bird calling you Jonny – Jonny."

"You shouldn't listen in on other people's conversations." He began to walk off nonchalantly.

"Hey, I asked you a question! Where are you goin'?"

Jonny halted. "Got to pick me brother up from playschool. I promised me mam."

"Yeah, that's what they all say. I left me bacon sarnie to get cold 'cos of you."

Jonny grinned and shrugged his shoulders complacently. "Sorry pal. Better hurry up and get back to yer sarnie then, eh?" He stepped away again but the labourer gripped his shoulder hard. Jonny looked down at the whites of his tattooed knuckles. "Get your hands off." He glared at the guy, who relaxed his grip. Jonny shook himself free and strolled off cockily. He caught a glimpse of Jackie watching him from the café window, shaking her head resignedly.

A meteor storm of kiddies and parents showered upon Jonny as he ducked and weaved towards his destination. The converted council row was besieged by Jason's playgroup Tuesdays and Thursdays; five year olds bouncing off the walls, trashing the place like faded seventies rock stars, that sort of thing. Jonny saw his little brother already, swinging on the iron railings, held in check by one of the playgroup supervisors in an appalling C&A suit. Jonny believed the diabolical dress sense of the teaching profession was one of the world's great, unanswered mysteries.

As Jason saw his older brother his face broke out into a hyperactive grin. The adult registered Jonny's presence and pressed an envelope into Jason's palm before scuttling off hurriedly down the road. Jonny thought this curious behaviour, but the sudden weight of Jason across his shoulders required his immediate attention.

"Whoah!" he yelled, pulling at the giggling ball of energy. "Christ, you weigh a ton!"

Jason slipped to the ground, punching big brother in the stomach on the way down. Jonny winced at a swipe dangerously close to his gonads. "Hey, be nice!" he protested. "Is this the way to treat your Jonny when you haven't seen him for weeks?"

It was true, and Jonny immediately regretted having said that. Jason was a smart kid and straight away picked up on the awkward truth. Since Jonny had moved down the road just a few miles, he was a sight for sore eyes in Old Swan.

"Mam says you don't wanna see us any more," said Jason immediately.

Jonny bent down and shunted Jason into his arms. "Nah, mam didn't say that really, did she?"

"Yes she did," said the boy emphatically. "And she said that you think you're too good for us now." Big eyes swallowed Jonny whole, his reflection wavering in their turquoise depths. "What's she mean, Jonny? Aren't you gonna come and play footie with me anymore?"

"Geroff! I'm dead chuffed with me family, alright?" Jonny kissed his brother's forehead and began to pull him across the road, clutching his little hand tight. He felt irritable that even a five year old could see through him. "I'm here now, aren't I?"

Jason looked up hopefully at him. "So can I have some footie stickers then?" he asked, pulling him to a paper shop.

"No ways."

"Dad says Germany are certs to win the Cup, too," he added knowledgeably.

"No they fuckin' won't!" He picked up speed, stomping his boots loudly. Jason struggled to keep up, tripping over his trainers, eyes fixed on his big brother beguilingly. Jonny avoided his gaze; he knew he had neglected his family, phone calls dwindling, Sunday roast replaced by Damon's packed lunch. Home was somewhere off Jonny's map and, fair dos, some were guilty on a grander scale – they avoided Liverpool full stop, mellowed their Scouse accent, ensconced themselves in their Notting Hill pied à terre. They might swear blind how proud they are of their roots, but get them to climb in their car and make the two-hour drive up the M1? No way.

To Jonny, Old Swan equated boredom, deprivation, and painful reminders of sexual frustration. He wished he saw things differently, but couldn't. Who would want to go back to that?

Little Jason was too young yet to know which way he was gonna go, thought Jonny grimly. It just took one spark – a teacher with an axe to grind, a best mate who was an apprentice nutter – and Old Swan had enough of those. The inner city waited, ready to pounce, impatient to dig its claws into his back when Jason finally fell on his arse. Jonny held tight onto his little, soft fingers, feeling that if he let go of the boy then that was it.

Carefree, swinging his arm, Jason dropped the letter he had been holding onto the ground. Jonny bent down to pick it up. "What's this about then?" he asked, examining it closely.

"It's for mummy and daddy," answered Jason, thinking it through. "A man gave it to me."

"One of your teachers?"

Jason shook his head. "Nope. From a man."

Jonny examined the plain paper envelope, addressed to his father. "What man? That fella I saw you with?"

Jason nodded. Jonny tried to swallow the dread that rose from the pit of his stomach. "He wasn't from your playgroup?"

Jason thought back carefully. "He said he was a friend of daddy's. He said give mummy and daddy the letter."

Jonny tore open the top end in agitation. Peering inside gingerly, he pulled out a single sheet of type, poorly transcribed on an old-fashioned machine. Some letters had smudged, while the paper was severely dog-eared. The message was simple, just a few lines long. Jonny weighed each icy word:

Down payment on loan received with thanks.
Outstanding amount payable immediately.
Failure to do so will result in physical harm to Jason.
This matter is non-negotiable.

Jonny dropped his arm to his side, ashen faced. He grinned weakly at Jason, who snuggled up to his leg and clutched, enamoured, at his thigh. "I'm hungry. Mam's doing fishcakes."

"That's nice," said Jonny, the words barbed in the back of his throat. He looked around in panic, clutching Jason hard against him.

The brown brick traffic junction turned its back, channelling its motor cars past and away in chrome arcs of movement. Lone pedestrians blanked out their surroundings in the haste to put their feet up and make a cup of tea. Jonny searched out some eye contact but the passers-by averted their gaze. Feeling like putting the world's integrity to the test, Jonny tried flagging down the nearest person. Jason stared up at him unblinkingly as he approached a lady veering dangerously towards pensionable age, dressed still in Silver Jubilee Year knitwear. She became aware of this open-faced youth making a beeline for her and immediately took off in another direction.

"Hey!" protested Jonny. "I just want to speak with you!" He quickened his pace behind the woman, who began to break into a trot in order to outrun him. "Go away!" she bleated. "Go away and leave me alone!"

Jonny scuddered to a halt. "Alright then!" He turned around in disgust. "Stupid cow!"

Jason raced up and took Jonny's hand. "Who was she Jonny? Who was she?"

"How do I know?" Jonny began to feel really stupid. "I just thought someone might be interested in our shitty problems."

Jason looked at him curiously. "Jonny's funny."

"Oh yeah?" Jonny put an arm around Jason's shoulders and gave him a squeeze. "Your brother's a big comedian." He craned his neck upwards, as though looking for guidance. Now, the afternoon sky was grey-tinged and non-committal, pressing down on their shoulders. For certain, they wouldn't get any help from up there.

"Come on," said Jonny resignedly, "let's get you home. We can have a game of footie." He stuffed the letter into his back pocket and crouched down to let his little brother ride piggyback on his shoulders.

Damon was the last to arrive, looking hot and flushed. Katy Ann piped up, "We know what you've been up to."

"Hush child," he blushed deep purple. "Anyway, chance would be a fine thing. Jonny's spending the day with his parents." He looked around bemusedly at the solemn gathering. "What's the big deal anyway? Why the secrecy? Why couldn't Jonny come along too?"

Gus motioned for Damon to sit on the pile of batik cushions at Sharma's feet. "Charlene thought it better to keep this very much between ourselves and not involve any outsiders yet."

"Charming," bitched Damon. "I must tell my beau how friendly me mates are." He flicked a glance at Serge. "Well, look what the cat brought in. And what have you been up to, to get Charlene's knickers in a twist?"

"What's that?" chipped in Gus. He was too wrapped up in his own problems to imagine that anyone else might also be shit-dodging.

Serge was about to open his mouth when Sharma intervened. "Now you leave him alone. It's just a few teething troubles and Serge is only staying with me until Charlene gets back." She shot a glance at Gus, who grimaced accordingly. "Staying with you, is he?" he grunted.

"That's right," said Serge breezily. "At night we play doctors and nurses, don't we Sharma?"

Damon looked askew at him. "You're disgusting. I didn't come here to discuss your sordid perversions."

"And what's so sordid about the idea?" protested Sharma. "Any more rampant misogyny from you boy and I'll set my daughter on you."

Katy Ann put up her fists and launched herself at Damon. The pair tumbled around in a fit of giggles.

Serge, dodging a flailing limb, sidled up to Gus. "Only joking," he whispered. "Maybe you have a better idea for a bed in the night? Know what I mean?"

Frankly, Gus didn't. He shook his head free of any loose wiring and clapped his hands officiously to restore law and order. "Alright, behave you lot! This is serious!" He tried to make himself heard over the horseplay, kicking Damon who wouldn't keep still.

"Ow, that hurt!" whined Damon. "What's your problem?"

"Well, if you let me explain, the sooner this will be over and you can get back to big boy."

Sharma nudged Damon in the ribs. "Is it true what they say then?"

"*Sharma!*" Gus threw up his hands in disgust.

"Well, get on with it," she grumbled.

Gus paced around the living room, evidently struggling to contain his agitation. They all wondered what was eating him; all knew how Gus was prone to the ravages of excess booze and speed, yet he looked corpse-like, grey-pale, bloodshot at the white of his eyes. They had never seen him look quite *so* rough before. When he spoke, it was hushed and heavy.

"Last night I… Well, you remember those morons that live on the corner of Huskisson Street?"

Serge's eyes flickered as the events of the other night came back to him.

"Do go on, darling," said Sharma. "Don't tell me they saw the error of their ways and signed up for a sex change?"

"Actually I sprayed 'Fuck off homophobic scum' across the front of their house and threw firecrackers through their window."

"Christ almighty!" exclaimed Sharma. "No horse heads under the pillow as well?"

"You took a risk," added Serge.

Gus let the trail of a smile ghost his face. "It was… fun. Don't tell me you've never wanted to do something like that? Felt so angry that you'd love to fuck up their lives instead of the other way round?"

Katy Ann nodded excitedly. "Our teacher Mr Williamson used to touch up me mate Kirsty. So we got him one day with laxatives crushed in his flask of tea. Well sorted."

"That's me girl," beamed Sharma. "But Gus, did anyone see you?"

Gus nodded glumly. "Looks like it."

"I saw you, all the racket you made," interjected Damon snottily. "So now what?"

"Now?" Gus suddenly sagged. "Now half of Toxteth is looking for me."

There was a stunned silence. Damon, Serge and Sharma exchanged glances. "What you gonna do mate?" asked Damon.

"Well, I sort of figure, if me number's up anyway, we might as well fight back."

Damon looked startled and began to fidget visibly. "Hello – *we?*"

Gus looked uncomfortably at the floor. "They've seen Serge for a start." He looked up at the handsome face with twinkling eyes glinting encouragement. Gus coloured with gratitude. "Guys, I'm really sorry, but Charlene has done some groundwork and it seems that since England lost to Germany on penalties there's talk of trouble. For a lot of people, kicking around a few faggots would be the perfect way to wind down on a hot summer's evening."

"I think this is more complicated than you think," said Serge sullenly.

"What do you mean?" asked Damon.

Serge cleared his throat. "Roxy was beaten up the other night, close from here. There was a big gang, waiting for him."

They looked sharply at him. "No!" gasped Sharma. "Is he alright?"

Serge shrugged. "I suppose. They take out the stitches today."

"We don't know it was gaybashing. It could have been his bad luck to be in the wrong place at the wrong time," said Damon.

"Don't we?" reasoned Serge. "One of Charlene's boys? Think about it."

"All the more reason to be ready for them when they come," said Gus.

Damon couldn't contain his impatience any longer. "But how are we going to fight back?" he exploded. "With our sharp dress sense?"

Gus regarded him coolly. "What are you going to do, Damon, if these guys catch up with you when you're walking home one night, alone?"

"Well, I don't know any more. And what are you going to do, Gus?" All looked up at this boy, orange hair zigzagging across a pale, freckly face. He suddenly looked very small. "I don't know either. But I hope to prevent it ever happening. Listen, Charlene's promised to muscle in if need be. Besides, this isn't gang warfare. I reckon if we just stand up to 'em a bit we might get a little respect and they'll leave us well alone."

"Damon's right," said Sharma carefully, "these guys don't mess around. I can't see what you can do against 'em. They're sadistic bastards."

"You, my darling, might be able to defuse the situation with a strategic shag here or there."

Sharma's jaw dropped. "Bloody marvellous! I get to be the Huskisson Street hooker! Am I supposed to wear 'em out before they go on the rampage?"

"Mam," said Katy Ann disapprovingly, "I don't want Uncle Gus beaten up. Jubilee would do it."

"Listen Gus," said Sharma after a moment's consideration, "I can see what you're saying and okay, it could be cool. God knows you all deserve respect and by dealing with these bastards now you're making it safer for Katy Ann when she grows up. But it's not worth ending up with your throat slit, is it mate?"

Serge stepped in. "I agree with Gus. If we are weak, then we make it easy for them. Maybe it's time we show our strength."

Gus made a mental note to forgive Serge for everything.

Damon couldn't disguise the contempt in his voice. "So what's the plan. Call them a few names? Criticise their hair styles?"

Gus flicked a viperous glance at Damon. "I reckon what we do is get the neighbourhood together, gay, straight — there are more than enough that would do it — and picket those queerbashers in Huskisson Street. I bet they put the word around with the gangs that I might be behind the other night. There's no one else who could have put two and two together to make four. I'm hoping it might be enough to scare 'em when they get up and see a hundred homophobe-hating freedom fighters threatening to do their heads in. Call the *Echo*. Fuck it — contact the dailies."

"Fuckin' brilliant," nodded Sharma vigorously. "I'm in!"

"Me too!" piped up Katy Ann. She grabbed Uncle Gus's hand.

Gus fiddled with the rings that jostled the knuckles on Katy Ann's little fingers. He felt empowered by the support of his mates. Curious how calamity can push and shove your life in constructive directions.

"I'm enrolling in gay self-defence courses down the community centre," continued Gus. "That's kind of optional. They're after me, really, so I figure that'll keep me out of harm's way and maybe improve me sex life. You never know." He mischievously eyeballed a nonplussed Serge.

Damon reluctantly succumbed to his friends' enthusiasm. He took a deep breath. "OK Gus, let's tackle this thing head on. I reckon a demo's a pretty smart idea."

Gus caressed Damon's cheek fondly. He recognised that his mate was high on Jonny and reluctant to come down. "Thanks pal. With a bit of luck that'll be the end of it and then we can get on with our lives." His eyes fell upon Serge who played unawares with Katy Ann.

Sharma pulled some hash cakes out of the oven and they settled down to watch Jarman's *Jubilee* on video. Gus's favourite film; resistance at least made sense then in a smug, stagnant Britannia. Had things turned out any better, 20 years later? This green and pleasant land seemed to spin eternally in some complacent time warp – perhaps it was the people who had changed, metamorphosing into house-proud Hitlers. Little England and its bleating sheep; turned your back and the sheep became a pack of wolves.

As the evening settled and bathed them in sulphurous pink light Charlene's angels grew strangely silent, unwilling to break the hushed intensity that enveloped them. It had been many months since they had all shared together like this. Adversity had crashed into them and scattered them like skittles; the 'Pool, confrontational, had boxed them into opposite corners. Gus and Serge, they used to be best mates and look at them now; Damon had long since turned to Jonny for a soul mate. The night ended light-headed in a group hug. As they pulled apart, they felt troubled. There seemed to lurk a dark finality in their goodbyes, the fleeting sensation of a door closing on their lives. The fears remained unspoken, however – something they would all regret for the rest of their lives.

7

"I SWEAR TO YER JONNY, on me mother's grave, that any fella, gay or straight, would like it up the arse given half the chance."

Jonny put down the well-thumbed copy of *Hello!* and looked at Phil resignedly. He really wasn't in the mood. He had enough to think about without indulging his workmate's train of thought. Mam had taken the letter with her habitual blind hysteria, while dad stoically retreated into that week's *Angling Times,* having sweet FA to contribute. Nothing new there. But Jonny was sure that the problem wasn't going to spirit itself away. Something had to be done before Herod started taking the proverbial first-born. So where were they going to get the cash? He couldn't ask Damon and wouldn't ask Charlene. He toyed with the idea of moving back home for a few weeks, until this thing had blown over. He knew this had been too good to last.

Jonny, in spite of himself, couldn't resist putting his workmate right. "Well for a start Phillys, your mam has yet to cop it or who else does your sandwiches every day? And speak for yourself mate. I've no desire to have anyone, or anything for that matter, up my bum."

Phil, 22, big-boned and losing his masculinity as fast as his hair, looked down at Jonny over his Camille Paglia reader. "Don't tell me darling you're still a virgin?"

"No, I'm a perfectly sane human being who likes being a top rather than a bottom, end of story."

Phil tutted. "The arse is just another sexual organ, not bloody Cheddar Gorge. You don't suddenly develop a limp wrist after the first time. Of course, the first time it may feel like a herd of elephants rampaging through there, but believe me love, before long a herd of elephants just isn't enough!"

Jonny shushed Phil as a middle-aged, bespectacled man in grey flannel walked in gingerly, attaché case under his arm. Phil looked him up and down disdainfully. "That'll be a tenner, love." The man fixed his gaze on the floor while handing over a crisp note in exchange for a key. Phil gave him an officious little smile. "Locker room's over there. You'll find a clean towel on your way through." Phil watched the man wander off nervously. He shook his head. "First time," he mouthed silently at Jonny. Then, not really interested if the man was out of earshot or not, he carried on speaking at normal volume, pitched somewhere between loud and unbearable. "Probably got a wife and two adorable little kiddies waiting for him at home. I'll give him ten minutes before he's dangling from the ceiling."

Jonny shrugged and clammed up. Phil, however, was having none of it. "I hear," he said, "that in New York the woman might strap on a dildo and fuck her boyfriend silly with it! Now that's what I call liberated! Of course in Knowsley we're way behind. In my neighbourhood the pet shop has to be under 24 hour surveillance or they'd all be there trying out the hamsters for size. Really! That's so passé! Even Richard Gere has moved on."

"Give it a rest, Phillys!" moaned Jonny. "God! I have to put up with this all day long when I work with you."

Phil gave him a hurt look. "Fine! Have it your boring way." He stared at Jonny hoping for a reaction, which he plainly wasn't going to get. "God you men are all the same!" he bitched. "You're as bad as me husband. As charming as a rattlesnake until you want to get your way and then it's darling-darling."

"Well be grateful that your Freddy takes an interest in that rancid little arse of yours!" Jonny's eyes twinkled, enjoying his off-the-cuff insult.

Phil clapped a hand to his mouth, feigning shock. "Hark at you! I've scratched people's eyes out for less." He sniffed. "Besides, won't take long for this boyfriend of yours to get fed up with the one-way traffic, if you get me drift."

"What do you mean?"

"Well there's no bigger turn off than a bloke with buns so flat you'd miss 'em if you blinked."

"I've a great butt, Phillys."

"What good does it do yer though, eh? As it is more shit comes out of your gob than your arse could ever come up with."

Jonny was lost for words. Phil mouéd in triumph and put his hands behind his head. "Oh dear Jonny. My talent is wasted on you, you know? When was queer anything else than a fancy way of saying your IQ's even smaller than your dick?"

"Me boyfriend's not complaining. Your Freddy meanwhile spends most of his time bitching about you."

"That's just his way of being affectionate. Don't worry Jonny, it's the quiet ones you should worry about."

They were distracted by the door swinging open to reveal another punter. "Oh my Lord," spluttered Phil. This one was *gorgeous*. Hair number one cropped, tapering to neat sideburns cradling intense azure eyes. Bambi skin to a voluptuous 'kiss me' mouth. Little designer chest hairs squirreled away between the Ben Sherman shirt collar.

"Good afternoon," said Phil primly. "Hello," the boy replied, but his eyes laser-beamed on Jonny.

Phil witnessed the electricity and rolled his eyes. "Here for the colonic irrigation?" he asked brusquely, throwing Jonny a viperous glance as he winced on the boy's behalf. "Shut it, *Phillys.*" Jonny tried not to blush under scrutiny.

"If your friend there is administrating it," answered the lad breezily. Jonny bowed his head so as not to burst out laughing.

"That's ten pounds and no backchat," chipped Phil abruptly. "Lockers over there and leave off the funny business or you're out on your ear. Next!"

The boy turned, but not before winking at Jonny. He watched the firm arse wiggle away, poured into 501s, and felt his dick twitch involuntarily.

"How'd yer like that," said Phil sourly. "Bloody cheek."

"You're right there. Look at 'em."

Phil looked sharply at Jonny. "The guy's a slut! He looks the sort that collects venereal diseases like other people collect stamps!"

"You're just jealous 'cos he fancied me, of course."

"Completely blind too. No taste in men." Phil smiled slyly. "Of course, your boyfriend would be very interested to find out what Jonny James gets up to at the office all day."

"Geroff! I'm as good as gold! There's no harm in a little flirting. You'd do it if anyone was desperate enough to fancy you."

"I'll have you know, I have them queuing up to ask me out." Phil leant back in his chair, picking his nose with his little finger. "But Freddy and I have something noble that you just wouldn't understand."

"Pays you, does he Phillys?" Jonny flicked Phil's finger out of his nose. "Lovely. Go much deeper and you'll come out the other end."

"You might take the piss Jonny James, but when you're a sad and lonely old queen on Otterspool seafront going for boys half your age I shall have the last laugh."

Jonny shrugged. "They say the beautiful die young, don't they?"

"That counts you out then frankly, doesn't it?"

Jonny smiled, almost feeling affectionate towards this slightly malformed, highly feminised queen. *Almost.* Still, he had to hand it to him. Phil deflected the prejudices of deepest, darkest England solely with his agile mind and sharp tongue. They had even once gone together to the local chippy with Phil swathed in a bright orange sarong and espadrilles like some fucked-up queer Hare Krishna with a foul mouth. Jonny had nearly died of embarrassment. Phil had nearly been thrown into a vat of chip fat but breezed out right as rain, not a put-down out of place.

Jonny rose and plopped himself demurely on Phil's lap. "What the fuck…!" beeped Phil in genuine astonishment. Jonny put his arms around his neck and began running his fingers through Phil's hair. "Well darling," he purred, "it looks like if no one else'll have me, you'll have to do." He leant forward towards the petrified Phil as if to kiss him.

"Eh geroff! Geroff!" Phil coloured deep crimson and flapped like a fish on land. Jonny slid off him in a fit of giggles. "Twat! I'm going to check on the sauna. See if I have to hose anyone down."

Phil fiddled with his ruffled hair. "If anyone needs hosing down it's you, you little pervert! And if you so much as lay a finger on the customers, the boss'll have you, you know!"

"I know, teacher's pet." Jonny yawned, then pouted mischievously. "Why don't you put something sexy on for me, when I get back? The boss said nothing about slap and tickle with your workmates…"

Phil's face nearly exploded with colour. "Oh fuck off! Leave me alone!" He affected a deep strop, arms folded, head turned away.

Jonny shuffled down the corridor, deliberately whistling loudly. He peeked first round the deserted locker room. The boss gave strict orders as to what was allowed in the sauna: body-to-body contact OK; oral sex OK; mutual wanking OK as long as things didn't get too messy. The local authorities turned a blind eye up to this point. Fucking *completely* out of the question – the council came down like a ton of bricks on infractions of this nature; licences revoked, courts brought in, financial ruin a dead cert. Things sometimes got pretty intense in the steam room and you almost needed two people to prise apart the interlocking bodies. Some didn't take kindly to having their fun spoilt, and reacted aggressively, but what the hell – they were naked. It didn't take long to embarrass them into good behaviour.

Jonny headed for the steam room. Wisps of vapour curled through the slightly vibrating swing doors. He carefully pulled them open and peered through, before stepping inside.

Jonny glanced around the room, screwing up his eyes. In one corner two figures enacted an elaborate sexual ritual. Jonny thought he recognised the civil-servant type on his knees, giving a blowjob to a large, beer-gutted man who gyrated his ample hips in naked pleasure. The civil servant slurped and cooed in obvious ecstasy, wiggling his rather miserable rump in the air. Jonny didn't like to be judgmental but the spectacle turned him stone cold, despite the debilitating heat. He opened another button on his shirt.

A hand descended over his eyes, slightly moist and smelling faintly of cock. A voice hissed in his ear, "Is that all you're going to do?" An unknown figure clamped himself to Jonny's back. He could feel what seemed to be a very large prick rubbing against his arse. "Here, let me help you." The figure began to fiddle at Jonny's belt. "This might come in useful later."

Jonny wriggled and freed himself from the stranger's strong grip. He spun around. It was the number one cropped lad that had eyed him up earlier, now consuming him even more lasciviously with his eyes. Jonny took a sharp intake of breath; this one was real stud material, he couldn't deny. His heart thundered in his chest and his groin began to swell in his pants. The bod that confronted him could be Damon's with the creases ironed out – designer hair tick-tacking across his chest and stomach, a dark sun tattooing his bellybutton; glistening thighs to bulging calves. Then, head up like an eager schoolboy, his thick, long cock; Jonny was no size queen but something like that could not be ignored easily.

"Jesus Christ," he whispered. "Hardly," answered the skinhead, who, with a smile playing across his lips, drew closer and unzipped Jonny's fly. Jonny's prick virtually lunged out of its Champion briefs like a wildcat. The skinhead saw it and tilted his head to one side, lips parted as if it were supper. He stepped forward and pressed his gleaming cocktip against Jonny's. "A welcome kiss," he said. "Now we've got the niceties over, do you want to fuck?"

Jonny swallowed hard. The skinhead was bent down before him, pulling Jonny's trousers and briefs to his knees. "Listen mate," said Jonny, trying to keep his voice steady, "you're just going to have to stop right there."

The skinhead looked up at him insouciantly. "Where? Here?" He took Jonny's cock full in his mouth, swallowing it whole. Jonny could feel his teeth skim the length of his hyper-sensitive dick, sucking furiously at his head. He bit his lip in order not to cry out and his eyelids fluttered, stonefree.

"Mmm, tastes nice," opined the skinhead between strokes, "spunk and sweat."

Jonny opened his eyes and looked down to see the lad going at his cock like a power drill, his hands mauling Jonny's balls, occasionally digging in beyond to his arsehole. Rough but effective. The skinhead's own fat prick swung untouched, a cold metal cockring hitching up his scrotum around his shaft which already dripped thick globules of pre-cum, hissing as they spattered the marbled floor. Jonny swayed, his head lolling on his shoulders like a worn-out punch bag, held aloft by the skinhead's seeing-to. He tried to focus across the room; the civil servant and his partner ogled him as if all their Christmases had come at once, advancing slowly as they pulled spiritedly at their dicks. Revulsion plummeted to the pit of Jonny's stomach. He heaved on the skinhead's forehead and pushed him off his cock, which jerked in the air as though it had lost its lifeline. "Leave it out!" he snarled.

The skinhead scowled viciously. "What the fuck did you do that for, eh?!" He raised a hand to grab at Jonny's cock and guide it back into his reddened mouth, but Jonny slapped it away. "Jesus mate, what's your problem?!" spat the skinhead this time.

Jonny raised his finger and jabbed it at them all, talking between clenched teeth. "Don't you come anywhere near me, OK? I've got a boyfriend. And, and – I love him. So just keep off, alright?"

Jonny glared at the skinhead, ready for a confrontation, but he was looking over Jonny's shoulder at some commotion happening behind him at the door. Irritated at the distraction, Jonny turned to see for himself what was going on. He nearly jumped out of his skin in shock.

This was turning out to be a hell of an afternoon.

Phil sat bored at the desk, fiddling distractedly with a pencil. He found his own company intensely tiresome; the last person he knew how to entertain was himself. In spite of this he could court the unlikeliest of company: Sally Army OAPs on a pub whip round; boozed-up Scallies with tattoos across their foreheads; heavily pregnant single mums on a mid-morning coffee break. In such unpromising circumstances Phil flourished. He would always come out on top with his self-deprecating wit and acid-precision insults. He gamely fulfilled the seaside special whoops, hows-your-father nostalgia that lurked at the heart of Britannia, even if wrapped up queer in an orange sarong. Perhaps his campness was the reassuring icing on the cake.

Phil fidgeted and consulted his watch sulkily. Where could Jonny have got to? Phil thought of the skinhead fluttering his eyelashes at Jonny like a bitch on heat. He shuddered. Phil was infatuated with his workmate and took Jonny's flirty indifference with a heady mix of masochistic despair and delight.

He stood up, dawdling momentarily, and then began to creep down the corridor that linked the little rabbit warren of restrooms, jacuzzis and steam baths hammered together in faux-Scandinavian pine. This building used to serve as an abattoir, hence the relative ease with which its culling chambers with draining ducts for blood and viscera were converted into imitation Hawaiian-palmed lagoons with piped music. The meat might be chewier, but the kill was as crudely effective.

Phil halted before the steam room, sensing instinctively the presence of figures behind its heavy doors. He approached gingerly and edged a finger through their middle. Steam puffed outwards as he leant forward and peered through the door crack. "Oh my giddy godfathers…" he muttered. Through the dense cloud he could see Jonny standing there hands-on-hips, trousers around his ankles and his very erect cock being hoovered by the crouching skinhead. That one seemed not in the least phased by Jonny's prick sliding vigorously down past his tonsils.

"The bastard!" Phil's knees almost derailed beneath him but he could not rip his eyes away from the orgiastic spectacle. He was skewered between tragedy and voyeuristic ecstasy, but he had to keep watching. None of Freddy's high-stacked porn videos at home were this horny. After one or two identikit scenarios with proto-sexual clones in a drugged-out haze, the celluloid thrill soon paled. This, however, was raw sexuality freeze-framed; emotional and bloody. Phil winced at the serious bodily harm Jonny seemed to be getting, but the boy appeared to be enjoying it.

Phil caught a movement out of the corner of his eye and swung his head in its direction. He nearly wet his pants at what he saw. "Shit, Mr Higgs!" The boss was striding towards him, puffing as he carried his hefty frame forward, dressed in ill fitting seventies plaid trousers and kipper tie on a sweat-soaked shirt that barely contained a swell of belly. Vertiginous sideburns cradled a rotund face sporting a lank moustache and spotty chin, even after forty-odd years. "Now Phillys," said Mr Higgs breezily, "I think you've been very much caught in the act."

Thank God he seems in a good mood, thought Phil. He removed his fingers from between the doors which lodged together again. "Sorry sir. I'll be getting straight back."

"I should think so too. Who's at reception? Where's Jonny?"

Phil's heart slipped a beat. "I think he went off to the bog, Mr Higgs."

His boss winced. "Bog? Toilet. Lavatory. Anything but bog, if you don't mind. Right, well get back to work." He winked furtively. "So what's happening in here then?" Mr Higgs went to open the doors, affecting a lewd grin.

"Nothing sir," interjected Phil hastily, "really. Just a couple of old codgers."

"Since when has necrophilia been up your street Phillys? I don't think so. Come on, out me way sharpish." Phil stepped aside reluctantly and Mr Higgs stuck his head round the door. Phil heard a muffled "Christ almighty" and then the door was thrust wide open. Phil saw over his boss's bulky frame the skinhead sprawling on the floor, eyeballing them arrogantly while the other couple backtracked rapidly. Jonny gaped stupidly at his boss, his cock swaying impressive in the disturbed air currents.

"What a pretty picture we have here Jonny James." Mr Higgs's eyes locked hard on his stricken employee.

"I can explain–"

"Save it lad! I think I'm intelligent enough to be able to figure this one out. Make yourself decent and then I want to see you in my office, right away!" He bowed to the clients in surreal decorum. "Sorry for the interruption gentlemen, please carry on." He spun round and out of the steam room, heels clicking down the corridor.

The hot air swirled as everyone stayed rooted to the spot. Phil's eyes darted across the plethora of naked flesh as if it were a spot-the-ball coupon. Jonny sighed and began wearily to pull up his briefs, crowning his resolutely stiff cock with difficulty. The skinhead vanished into the steam as though he had never existed.

"Hells bells Jonny, that's it. You're out, I tell you." Phil was pulling at Jonny's trousers as he hoisted them up over his waist. "That's alright Phillys, I think I can dress meself," said Jonny quietly.

"Sorry." Phil stepped back, anguish etched onto his features. "Why'd you do it, eh?"

Jonny eyeballed him. "Do what? If you want to know I had it all under control."

Phil's mouth twitched at the corners. "Really? I think I see. You burst in with your knickers around yer ankles and shouted 'Nobody move, this is a stick up!'?"

Jonny frowned and then burst out laughing. He leant over and then planted a kiss on Phil's forehead. "Yeah mate, something like that." His smile vanished just as quickly. "Just a minute Phillys. What were you doing here anyway? You weren't telling tales to Mrs Merton out there were you?"

"No mate! No way! He just caught me," Phil blushed vermilion, "watching you at it through the door."

Jonny smirked. "Oh were you now?" He suddenly looked solemn. "I think your sort are disgusting."

Phil virtually shrieked in shame. "Oh God Jonny! I'm really sorry! What – what are you laughing for?"

"God, you're so bloody easy to wind up. Come on it's fucking hot in here. You smell like a rat's arse already!"

They stepped outside into formica cool. Jonny sucked in a deep breath. "Well, here I go to get me six of the best." He shook Phil's hand ceremoniously. "Phillys, see yer in the next life."

"Oh don't, I hate goodbyes." Phil's eyes glistened. "I get like this seeing Freddy off to work every day."

"You're just afraid he won't bother to come back one day." Jonny dug him in the ribs and planted a big kiss on Phil's lips.

"Cheeky!" Phil looked at his mate. "You know, if you can't hold a job down in a bloody sauna Jonny, what can you do?"

Jonny tried to brush away the remark with his customary bravado. "Merseyside is the land of opportunity Phillys, haven't you heard?"

"For crack dealers and second-rate comedians maybe, love."

"Well there you go. That's two options for a start." Jonny beamed disarmingly. "Now let me get sacked before you start looking me another job, alright?"

He strode off confidently down to Mr Higgs's office, blowing Phil a kiss.

Jonny braced himself and rapped on the door. "Come in," he heard from inside, muffled.

Mr Higgs office was plain and featureless, devoid of furniture bar desk and chair, while a large metal filing cabinet loomed starkly in one corner. It was remarkable for one thing though; lined against all four walls were piles of gay porn magazines. They jostled together like some Manhattan skyline of garish, fuzzy colour. Phil and Jonny had often joked about what Mr Higgs got up to when he disappeared, sometimes for hours, into here, his inner sanctum. Jonny sniffed and struggled not to gag on the stale, decrepit odour that stung his nostrils.

"Right Jonny, sit down." Mr Higgs indicated the empty chair facing him. Jonny saw that his boss had some porn rag in his hands as he was speaking to him. Though upside down, he briefly glimpsed full-page cock shots, ejaculating over the double spread.

He sat uneasily, goose pimples rising at the feel of the imitation leather seat. For a good minute, Mr Higgs ignored him as he fidgeted, instead flicking through the remainder of the magazine.

An open spread was suddenly flung before Jonny onto the desktop, making him jump. He saw a teenager, skinny and pale, pinned by two fat cocks that forced their way between his jaws. He looked from that to Mr Higgs, slowly.

"Nice eh?" His boss was grinning from ear-to-ear. "What do you think of that then, Jonny?"

The boy paused, wondering where this conversation was leading. He chose his words carefully. "I think this lad's gonna wish he'd kept his mouth shut."

Mr Higgs roared with laughter, in fact he laughed so much that tears rolled down his cheeks. He wiped them away with his thumbs as he still sniggered in jerks and spasms. Jonny considered bolting for the door.

"Very funny, me lad! This isn't about you now, is it? I suppose this is the moment when you give me some ridiculous explanation for why you had your cock down the throat of that lad back there."

Jonny opened his mouth to speak and Mr Higgs raised his blotchy hand to silence him. He suddenly looked very stern. "Save it lad. I can't really have my staff participating in the hi-jinx these dirty little buggers get up to, can I? Do you really want me to lose me trading licence for your irresponsibility? That wouldn't be very fair would it?"

"I'm sorry Mr Higgs, it won't happen again—"

"You're bloody right it won't. As of now, you're sacked. Collect your stuff and be out with you."

"Oh." Jonny had been expected this but his nerves still crashed to the floor. "What – what about me wages?"

"I can't be bothered right now. Come and pick them up next week." Mr Higgs's face was buried in another magazine he had pulled out from a desk draw.

Jonny stood up, smarting as if punched in the stomach. He had been expecting this but he was still proud. He didn't like being pushed around by some tosser and was well aware that there was fat chance he would see his wages. He was making for the door when Mr Higgs called out again.

"Wait a minute Jonny." He pulled himself out of his chair and lumbered over to Jonny, breathing thickly. The stale smell followed him across the room. His shadow loomed over the boy. Jonny felt a hand snake round and begin to caress his arse.

"Jonny, I like you. I really do. You're a good lad. I could find it in myself to give you a second chance, you know."

Here we go, thought Jonny. Mr Higgs's hand whipped round to his crotch, which began to get a hefty grope.

"What – do you mean?" A knot tightened in the back of Jonny's throat.

"I mean if you play your cards right, your job might still be here for you. Or, you never know, I might even have a nice little opening lined up for you elsewhere. This isn't my only line of business, as you can well imagine." Mr Higgs hand was now trying to frigg Jonny vigorously through his trousers. He pulled himself free and glared up at this sweaty brute.

"I think you'd better keep your hands to yourself, or the council might really have something to say about this place, you dirty bastard."

Mr Higgs whisked his hands away and took a step back. "You ungrateful little prick. Go on, get the fuck out of here! Out!" A little, nervous muscle twitched furiously over his eyebrow.

Jonny regarded Mr Higgs disdainfully. "You're a bloody disgrace." He strode out and slammed the door behind him. Emerging into reception, Phil stared at him in bemusement. "My God, Jonny! You look like you've been a week in Torremolinos. I'd die to get that colour."

Jonny leant against the wall, feeling queasy. "Listen Phillys, do us all a favour and torch this place when I'm gone, eh?"

"Oh dear. So you didn't get the promotion then, eh?"

"If I'm gonna go up in the world mate, it's not gonna be by having it off with any dirty old fucker that takes a fancy to me."

Phil gawped as Jonny grabbed his rucksack and made for the door. "Yerwhat? No… *No!* Jonny! Jonny! Wait up!"

He was already out the door, chasing a bus vrooming into town.

8

10PM ANY SATURDAY, witness the stroppy, gilded rush of amphetamine ambition in a concrete wasteland, the hemmed in Ecstasy danger and silly-Scally tomfoolery laced with hate that is Liverpool city centre. The plethora of bars, pubs and clubs form a backbone left to right, curling around the Mersey. Discobright attractions at the head – Cream, Voodoo, Baa Bar, MelloMello. Legendary runts and fagland aspiration at the tail – the Escape, the Lisbon, the Curzon, while Garlands jostles uncomfortably with the State and its hordes of neanderthals. Gus plunged headlong into the freaky promenade, smelling of sherbet and looking like something beautiful the cat had brought in. On his arm tra-la-laaed Noreen, who at her age should know better; polyestered school dinner lady by day, she became a *Faster Pussycat! Kill! Kill!* fantasy by night, only given away by the stretchmarks. Gus liked Noreen because she was *always* in it for the crack when most 45 year old housewives were already tucked up in bed; she liked Gus because he was a surrogate son who could keep up with her diet of pills and vodka. Her real children were a massive disappointment to Noreen, quietly filed under respectable, hardworking and cut-throat middle class.

They clattered downtown turning heads and stomachs but they couldn't care a fuck, seeking out that knowing look, that quick, appreciative smile to say they had pulled it off, *just*. Tonight was the Garlands all-nighter, a desperate Scouse manoeuvre to rival Manchester swank in a dingy pub setting, yet it worked. The music policy might be handbag – Jamiroquai, Brand New Heavies, Livin' Joy – but reach inside and you pulled out a loaded revolver.

The crowd might be mixed; still at least the straight boys took their shirts off, eager to please.

Gus got in for free because he was the talk of the town, the orange-topped crusader who had pissed on the queerbasher's firework. There was a buzz in the air, a sense of expectancy of better days to come. Gus wanted to partake in the euphoria but he saw beyond the fanfare into a troubled future. Thrown unwillingly into the spotlight, dodging well-wishers and autograph hunters, he reacted with humility and installed himself in a dark corner with Noreen and some mates, swigging on bottled water.

Noreen raised her eyebrows at the sight of that over her habitual double vodka with a twist. "Goin' a bit hardcore, aren't you love?"

"I've taken an E tonight and I'm bracing meself in case Prince Charming makes a move."

"You mean the Ice Queen is still hanging around for scraps?" That was Terrance, Mancunian by birth, Scouse by vocation. He was always bitchy about Serge because he was resolutely ignored.

"Sssh!" motioned Noreen. "Gus'll give you a fat lip if you're not careful. Looks like he's moving in for the kill. Blood and sequins everywhere."

"Oh how wonderful!" exclaimed Pamela, whose real name had been forgotten by all but his family. "I'm fully in favour of blood sports."

"When *was* the last time you got your end away, Gus darling?" asked Terrance, adding insult to injury.

"Wasn't it that lavatory attendant from Leeds, over a year ago?" recollected Pamela. "He only got a hard-on by licking the toilet bowl, didn't he?"

"Geraway!" shrieked Noreen. "Did you get his number? I could do with him for my bog ever since a tampon lodged up there last month."

"Look I weren't to know," protested Gus, somewhat exasperated. "He had a pierced eyebrow and looked like

Ewan McGregor! Now do me a favour. Just be good mates and keep out me way when the time comes, eh?"

"Don't you worry, I'll put them on their leads," said Noreen.

"Anyway," scowled Gus, "you two are hardly flavour of the month when it comes to getting laid."

Pamela pulled out a little compact mirror from his pocket and scratched a tiny yellowhead that throbbed at the corner of his mouth. "I am keeping myself for Mr Right."

"Listen love," said Noreen, "you're daft if you think you'll ever get your end away with your boss at work. He's married with two kids fer Chrissakes!"

Terrance leant over, indicating Pamela. "He's convinced he's in with a chance ever since the Christmas work's party where he got a subscription to *Chat* magazine as a prezzie."

"Pity the poor heterosexual who tries to be gay-friendly," sighed Gus. "It always ends in tears."

"Anyway, it's hardly our fault if we've slept with everyone worth sleeping with in the 'Pool," said Terrance. "Where have all the fuckers got to? It's enough to send you off to London in desperation."

All gasped in horror and made a crucifix symbol in Terrance's face. "Back, evil one!" hissed Pamela.

"Don't ever mention that horrible, horrible place again!" grimaced Gus. "The only good thing about Londoners is that the dirty little buggers never venture this far north. Alright, I think I'm gonna have a dance. You two are doing me head in." Gus made to stand up when he saw Serge emerge through the main door, paying his entrance fee. "Oh God, he's here. He's here. What do I do?"

"Not whatever it is you're doing right now love," said Terrance. Gus was twitching like he had ants in his pants, clenching and unclenching his sweaty palm. Noreen took one hand and gave it a consolidatory squeeze. "Relax eh?" She wondered whether the E had been a good idea, but knew that otherwise Gus could be as spiky as a porcupine.

"Oh God he's seen me. He's coming over…"

Serge sauntered into Gus's arms, planting a hot, tender kiss on his dry lips. "I am very happy to find you here," Serge whispered in his ear. "Hiya Noreen, hiya lads."

"Hiya Serge," they chorused. Serge looked down at them, detecting a curious inflection in their voices. "Alright then, eh?" he said hesitantly. Noreen, Terrance and Pamela nodded fervently, staring up at him.

There was a moment's silence. "Oh look Terrance, your lipstick's smudged," said Pamela suddenly, nudging him savagely in the ribs. Terrance squealed and had turned to give his mate an earful when he finally caught on. "Good God! Get me to the powder room – and fast!" He rose, pulling up Pamela and Noreen with him by the scruff of their necks. "Excuse us boys. Serge, ask him about sanitary hygiene in the home. It's fascinating!"

Noreen gave Gus a sly peck on the cheek as she passed. "Good luck," she whispered.

Serge watched the three of them sashay towards the dance floor. He shook his head in bemusement. "What was that about?"

Gus managed a sheepish grin. "Oh, nothing." He motioned Serge towards the bar. "Fancy a drink?"

"My round. I have a bit of cash for doing a model shoot for Everton football gear. You hear about that?"

"Someone might've mentioned it." Really all Gus wanted was to rip off Serge's Martin Margiela T-shirt and loop the loop on his body.

"I was in Oxfam on Smithdown Road when comes this bloke to say he is from a model agency. An hour later I have two hundred quid for looking good in a pair of shorts."

Gus could well imagine how good Serge looked. "Did you get any backstage passes for the Everton changing rooms?"

"No."

"Then I'm not impressed."

Serge laughed and put an arm around Gus's shoulders. He was immediately aware of the boy responding to his touch, sinking into his grip. He looked cheekily at Gus. "You're a bit more nice to me today."

Gus shrugged his shoulders, surprised himself too, with the resumption of normal service after he had typically hit the panic button. He felt calm, assured and unafraid of Serge. "I took an E so…"

Serge's expression clouded. "Well I can't be expected to get through Mariah Carey remixes till 6am without a little bit of divine intervention," added Gus hastily.

"I just once like to see the real you, you know – without make-up or chemicals." Serge brought a hand up to Gus's cheek and stroked it softly. "It is important to me. I'm sure inside that little monster is… a fluffy bunny."

Gus groaned in mock-horror and giggled nervously. "Geroff! Whatcha wanna see the real me for? You'd be slitting yer wrists in boredom."

Serge took Gus's hand in his own. "No I wouldn't. How about I take you to dinner to prove you are wrong? Just you and me – no additives. Just my company for stimulation."

Gus's heart roared in his chest. He brandished his water weakly and croaked, "This is finished." Serge grinned broadly. "I'll get you another one then." He disappeared off to the bar.

Terrance rocketed up to Gus spitting fire in his wake. He threw a contemptuous glance at Pamela who followed a few paces behind. "God that little tart is about as welcome as a boil on your bum!"

Gus brought himself out of his stupor. "Why, what's he done?"

"Well I get this nice gentleman coming over and starting to chat me up, when this one starts revealing intimate details about me anatomy at the top of his voice."

Pamela stopped within inches of Terrance's face, glaring furiously at him. "I think he has the right to know you've got three testicles before you've got him strapped to the bed and there's no escape for the poor lad."

Gus clapped a hand over Pamela's mouth. "Shut your fat gob will yer! I should think most people in Garlands heard that!"

Pamela waved his hand dismissively. "Believe me, most people know already. Have you heard the latest? "Terrance's tackle is so scary, Liverpool are thinking of signing him up for the league!"

"God, you're a mean bitch!" spat Terrance.

Gus sighed wearily. "With friends like you, why am I worrying about queerbashers?" He looked from one to the other, angry at their insincerity. "I'm fed up with the lot of you. Why don't you piss off, Pammy, until you get your attitude seen to?"

Pamela gawped, gobsmacked at having received the red card after a lifetime's carte blanche. Gus squared up to him, resolute and stern; Terrance held his breath, fascinated by the spectacle. Ashen-faced, Pamela spun on his heels and made straight for the door without a word to anyone.

Gus let out a deep breath. "Jesus that was a bit harsh!" gabbled Terrance.

"You think so?" Gus winked at Serge as he was handed a fresh water. "If anything these past few weeks have made me question a lot of things – behaviour like that for example. I can take a bit of leg pulling but that was pretty despicable, eh?"

"What do I miss?" asked Serge.

"Nothing worth you wasting your time on, mate."

"Oh come on!" scowled Serge. "You always have the gossip to yourself!"

"I'd watch him, love," said Terrance reprovingly. "I think all his success has gone to his head." He disappeared into the throng that choo-chooed between Garland's two rooms.

"Well how do you like that?" grumbled Gus. "I stick up for him against Pamela and he's pissed off with me!"

Serge shrugged. "Why doesn't that surprise me? Shit sticks to shit, remember?"

"Those two have elevated the put-down to an art form. It's bloody scary."

"Well, it's good they are gone. This is now a bitch-free zone." Serge placed an arm around Gus's waist and gave it a hearty squeeze.

"I'm not so sure about that, buster. Remember how you always used to have a go at me for me dress sense?"

"Oh yes. Those see-through plastic trousers and no underwear. It was bloody dangerous to walk the streets of Liverpool with you."

Gus smirked fondly at the memory. "Well, I've calmed down now," he whispered in Serge's ear. "Still not wearing underwear though."

Noreen sidled up to them both, dragging an unwilling, broad-shouldered teenager with her. "Sorry to barge in fellas! Gus, I was wondering when you're gonna have a boogie? The dance floor's pretty dull without you."

Gus kissed her affectionately. "I'll be right with you." He indicated Noreen's company. "And this is?"

"Oh yes! Me nephew. I found him hiding from me in a corner. Says he's not a fag, of course, but who'd believe that, eh? Dan, I'd like you to meet two of me favourite poofs, Gus and Serge."

"Hiya," said Gus, "I bet you weren't expecting to see Aunty Noreen here, was yer?"

Dan shook his head in embarrassed silence, while Serge studied him intensely. "Funny," said Serge, "I'm sure I recognise you from somewhere."

"Oh do tell!" shrieked Noreen. "I'd do anything for a bit of scandal in me family!"

"Sorry mate," interjected Dan quickly, "never seen you before in me life."

Serge couldn't place him, it was true, though the soft, adolescent contours of Dan's face rang distant bells in the back of his mind. "I'll remember. What about Terrance? He went off in bad mood to the dance floor."

"Since you ask about him," said Noreen, "it seems a lad won't leave him alone, very curious to see what he has down his trousers. He's so insistent, I nearly had to mace him. Am I missing something here?"

Gus's eyes twinkled. "Terrance has got a lot of balls, love."

Noreen looked quizzically at Gus. "You've lost me. Anyway I don't have time for riddles today." She grabbed onto Dan's arm. "I've got to find a boyfriend for me nephew here." Dan opened his mouth to protest but Noreen whisked him away before he could utter a sound.

"I love her!" enthused Gus, struggling to be heard over the whoops from the dance floor as a clubland favourite was aired. "She's so fabulous!"

"I think I remember her nephew, too," said Serge. "I'm almost sure I had him in the bushes at Otterspool not too long ago."

"Spare me the gory details please."

Serge coloured. "I know. I know." He raised his hand as though to take a vow. "I promise, no casual sex until after our dinner date. And I hope you know that is very difficult for me. You're hard work, Gus, but I will do my best."

"I set me standards very high," Gus gave Serge a coy kiss, wondering whether he was at all aware Gus would sell his soul to the Devil for as little as a lock of Serge's hair. "Fancy a dance, sexy chops?"

They manoeuvred through the scattered clumps of gay flora and fauna to the dance floor: skimpy youths with concave chests, arms skyward in disco delirium; bare breasted Scally boys with pert, button nipples, scouting for sugar daddies; sullen couples bordering the action in matching clubwear, muscle shirts, Diesel and Dr Martens. Clusters of day-glo girlies jigged on the spot, oblivious to the sneers of boozy lesbians but basking in the admiration of glamour-starved queer boys.

A hand tugged at Gus's shoulders. He turned to see a friend of Damon's whom he only knew by sight. The face was open and friendly. "Alright lads? Me name's Simon. Gus mate, I'd like to give you a big kiss." He grinned at Serge. "You don't mind, do you?"

"Be my guest." He relinquished his grip on Gus who squirmed as he was given a wet, slurpy kiss on the lips. "Crikey, what was that for?" puffed Gus.

"You, mate, are an inspiration to us all! Thanks to you I really told this tosser where to get off."

"His name wasn't Terrance, was it?" asked Serge. Gus shooshed him.

"Eh? There I am, eyeing up this gorgeous guy, queer as fuck in a Superman T-shirt cut off at his bellybutton. Or so I thought, seeing him wiggle his garden path at me like it were his crack in need of polyfilling. I look at him, he looks at me, right? So's I go up to him and start chatting him up and then he gets all shirty with me. "I'm not a poofter, I'm from Bradford," he says, "so fook off!" Well, I thought, I'm not having this – what's he doing here in a gay club if he can't even be civil? We're not some bloody freakshow. So I clock 'im one, the bouncers come over and I get him chucked out."

"Wicked!" said Gus. "I, for one, have had enough of these straight lads gatecrashing our clubs 'cos we're in *The Face* and then hassling us 'cos it's all too queer for their liking."

"The girls are alright," said Serge, "they're dead funny sometimes."

Gus frowned. "Yeah, but that's one reason why we get these straight lads here, looking to pull."

"I don't want 'em anywhere near me," concurred Simon.

Gus slapped him on the back, revelling in his new ally. "So I can count on you to be at the demo next week, Simon?"

"You can bet your life on it pal!" Simon winked at Gus, indicating Serge. "Now, is he yours, or can anyone have a go?"

"I loan him out, but he don't come cheap."

Simon frisked Serge lustily with his eyes. "I'll have to start saving up me pocket money then. Nice to meet you finally Gus, Damon's always got a good word for you."

"Cheers, my dear." Gus gave Simon a little wave as he dived onto the dance floor. "What a nice boy," he said.

"Good taste in men, I think," teased Serge.

"If your ego gets any bigger you won't fit through the door, mate." Gus reached down and cupped Serge's crotch in his palm. Through denim Gus felt a hot prick swell responsively to his touch.

"And if this gets any bigger…?" asked Serge slyly.

"This?" replied Gus, sensing his own loins tingle. "This we'll just have to put to bed till the swelling goes down." Gus couldn't believe himself, sounding for the entire world like some sex line vox pops. Serge seemed to like it in any case, placing all his weight firmly onto his crotch in Gus's tight grip. Trailing a finger down Gus's chest, he said, "I'd like to do you now Gus, on the bar, but dinner first. I want to prove to you there's more to Serge Mihajlovic than the thing in my trousers."

"Uh – OK." Gus tried to stem the flurry of pornographic images that zoomed through his mind. He had kind of hoped they could skip the preliminaries. "Are you asking me out, soldier?"

"I might be."

"Fair enough." Gus faltered, tongue-tied. Wonderboy here had really foxed him this time. The last thing Gus had expected was Serge soft and gentle. Gus had braced himself to win him over with guile, panache and cunning strategy. He had even polished his nipple ring, though all that did was make it go a bit septic.

As it was, he could only imagine Serge lying buck-naked by his side, stretching out across Gus's body and kissing his nipple better with his soft, capable lips. Gus squirming in pleasure with the tingle of his teat being sucked up into shape, as he reached down to Serge's fat cock, squeezing it against his own, ready to share hot bodily fluids. Like a little boy scout, ready for anything.

9

THE PROSTITUTE SHUFFLED DISCONSOLATELY across the street in Primark slingbacks. Pencil skirt holding lumpen knees at bay, orange crocheted top suffocating massive breasts. Hair, dark split ends with a gaslight sheen. Eyes surprisingly soft hazel, but stung, confrontational. Tonight it was cold, a chilly breeze blowing from the north, the black velvet sky spattered with stars. She lit a cigarette and dragged deep on its bitterness. Business was slow – only one trick all day. The streets were quiet and still, save the urban tumbleweed of loose newspaper sheets rolling down the hill.

Damon and Jonny came to a halt on the other side of the road to her, on their way home from a boozy night at the Curzon. The dingy, uncharismatic vault had benefited no end from its recent cameo in *Priest* at the flicks. Most nights it was chocka with scraggly middle-agers and shrill youngsters, heads almost obliterated by the thick pea-souper of cigarette smoke that descended from the ceiling. Damon and Jonny had become addicted to its shameless, classless, legless ambiance of homosexuality from the Dark Ages. Gus sneered at their lack of disco ambition but, anyway, they thought Garlands was just mutton dressed as lamb – and maybe they were right.

They waved cheerfully as they recognised the dour-faced prostitute. "Hiya Molly."

Her expression brightened. "Alright lads? How are me little lovebirds?"

"Oooh Molly, he's wonderful." Damon flicked his head in Jonny's direction. "I don't have to lift a finger."

"He's very much lady of the manor," added Jonny.

"The best ones are always queer, love. You don't have to tell me anything. I've been doing this long enough to figure that out." Molly stabbed the cigarette butt out on the pavement with her foot. "I'm calling it a day boys. Liverpool manhood is a bloody disgrace these days. And him indoors'll be screaming for his supper by now after the evening shift."

"See ya Molly." They watched her massive body shuffle into the darkness. Damon turned round and craned his neck up, feeling subdued by her shadow. The Anglican cathedral pierced the night sky, a slab of granite foreboding. "Why don't they keep the lights on all night? It looks fucking ugly." He shivered.

"That's the whole point," said Jonny. "It's meant to scare the shit out o'yer. The Godsquad are a load of bloody fascists, if you ask me."

Damon raised his eyebrows. "What happened to the nice little Catholic boy yer mam thinks she's got for a son?"

"Dunno. Must be the company I keep." Jonny smiled and slipped his arms around Damon's waist.

They stood together in silence for a few minutes, lost in their own thoughts. Jonny could sense Damon was troubled.

"What's the matter, darling?"

Damon disentangled himself from his lover. "I was just thinking about this place. We spend our lives sticking up for it, saying we're proud to be Scousers, that it's the best place in the world. But what's it fucking ever given us, eh?"

Jonny grimaced. "This is that business with Gus again, isn't it? Look the demo's next week. That should sort things out."

"You really believe that? I'll bet you anything that things'll get worse before they get any better. Anyway, what have you got to be so cheerful about? After what your family's been goin' through…"

Jonny chewed on his bottom lip; with Damon in this mood he dreaded having to own up to his double dose of bad news. "I've got you to give me something to look forward to."

Damon glowered. "Yeah well – fuckin' dump." He wedged his fingers obstinately into his jeans.

Jonny looked at Damon intensely. "Eh now misery guts! This is our home. We're gonna build a life together here. Okay the 'Pool's full of nutters but that's one of the best things about it. It's one of the few places left in this gutless country with anything down its trousers. That's why it's always gonna be different, and special."

"If you say so."

Jonny took Damon in his arms again and gave him a long, passionate kiss. He brushed Damon's hair away from his face and grinned reassuringly. "Yes I do. Come on. I'll show you Scousers make the best lovers, too."

They turned into Huskisson Street, its Georgian terraces descending far into the distance. To Jonny it was beautiful – anything was better than Old Swan. Yesterday he and Damon had applied together to a housing association for a new flat in a refurbished house off Sefton Park. Dead posh. With any luck they could be moving in within a couple of months; Jonny hoped it would take Damon's mind off his temporary retreat to his folks, if he actually got round to telling him. It made it seem kind of official, their relationship. Funny, ever since he was a little kid he'd dreamt of this, in one of those genderless fantasies that grip young imaginations. He'd shacked up with gym teachers, swimming instructors and even the milkman – he was a busy little bee. He kiss-chased little girls across the playground as boys do, but his mind was elsewhere. Now, the fantasy was flesh and blood named Damon, the ambition true and signatured in blue ballpoint on council application forms. Funny – despite everything, Jonny couldn't imagine ever being happier than this.

"Babe…?" he turned and placed his hands on Damon's shoulders. "Look – I've got something I have to tell you."

"What's that?" Damon looked up at him guilelessly. For a moment Jonny panicked, uncomfortable with the blind puppy dog infatuation that confronted him. Damon was a blank slate on which Jonny could impose any fantasy, if he so wished, and Damon would accept it without question. He breathed Jonny, he was Damon's life. Jonny could see that, in the innocent acceptance in his boyfriend's stare. He had no intention to hurt Damon, but warning bells rang in the back of his mind.

"I was sacked from the sauna yesterday."

Damon frowned. "What happened?"

Jonny took a deep breath. "Me boss caught me with a customer." He flicked a nervous glance at Damon. "I'm sorry. I'm really sorry."

"Oh." Damon avoided Jonny's gaze, face pale.

"Listen babe. I know I did wrong and I'm not making excuses. The lad really caught me out, I barely laid a finger on him. It's just that – what he did to me, well I didn't exactly try to stop him either, y'see…"

Jonny could see emotion cloud Damon's face and he squirmed. "I don't want to lose you," said Damon quietly.

Jonny gathered him up into his arms. "Baby, you're not going to lose me ever. Don't start crap like that eh? This won't happen again, never."

Damon looked at his lover steadily. "You don't know what I'd do if I didn't have you any more, Jonny. You have no idea."

Jonny tried to laugh off Damon's intensity. "If you come at me with anything sharper than a butter knife I'm off like a shot. I don't want you getting any ideas after that Bobbit fella lost his knackers. My todger's not ending up on nobody's mantelpiece."

Jonny trailed his fingers down to Damon's palm and interlocked hands. "Look," he began uncertainly, "there's something else. I'm gonna have to go back to me parent's place for a couple of weeks."

Damon flexed. Jonny could feel his boyfriend's fingernails dig into his flesh. "Like you decide to tell me this *after* goin' for a new flat?" Damon's eyes seared his discomfort with an I-knew-this-was-too-good-to-last-you-bastard expression written over his face.

"It's only till things calm down," added Jonny hastily. "They've made threats about harming little Jason. I can't let anything happen to me brother – you know that, right?"

"Just shut it, for fuck's sake! I don't want to hear another word," said Damon fiercely. He trembled against Jonny as he pulled him into a secluded alleyway. Garages lined up on either side, descending into darkness. Damon scrutinised their surroundings, his eyes alighting on a nearby skip that afforded some privacy. "I want yer to make love to me, right here." He began scrabbling at the buttons of Jonny's Levis.

"Yerwhat?! Can't you wait till we get home, at least?"

"I need you…"

"Jesus!" Jonny felt his prick harden against Damon's thigh. He looked round nervously. "It's too dangerous."

Damon's voice was thick with desire. "Then live dangerously." He pulled out his cock and placed it in Jonny's hand. It throbbed with hot blood. Jonny looked wildly at Damon and could resist no longer. Damon was pushed up against the skip, piled high with rubble. He gasped, the wind knocked out of him. Debris trickled onto the cobbled street, clattering loudly. "Sorry…"

"Just do me, Jonny."

Jonny kissed at Damon's open throat shimmering milky-white in the halogen sky. His hands raced over Damon's soft chest hair beneath his Comme des Garçons shirt, the boy's chest heaving. Damon fiddled at his shirt buttons, thrusting his cock against Jonny's groin while pulling him closer. They kissed in starlit fever, sucking hard at their tongues. A sheen of perspiration sparkled like wet dew on their straining bodies. Their naked skin flexed, every pore open and greedy to touch. Jonny too unbuckled and let his trousers slip to his knees, his prick energised. "I love you," he gasped.

"I know." Damon stepped back and descended to Jonny's crotch. "Oh, you have a beautiful cock. Just think what that's done to me these last few weeks." He stroked it in awe.

Jonny cupped Damon's balls in his hand. "Then see to it." Their eyes met and they grinned at each other. "Go on." He leant back and gasped as Damon's lips closed over his shaft. Pleasure ached in the muscles of his stomach. His nipples, hard in the chill air, snagged his corduroy shirt hanging half off his shoulders. He closed his eyes, head skywards, lost in a wet kiss, in a syrupy lick of sensation. His fingers tugged at Damon's hair, caressing the boy's smooth, sienna skin at the nape of his neck, skin descending into the shoulder muscles beneath his shirt and then to deeper pleasure. Damon seemed like a man possessed, swallowing Jonny's cock to the hilt. He guided the motion with his hands dug into Jonny's arse, faster then slower, steadying his lover with his soft lips embracing tender cocktip. He sensed the rising urgency in Jonny's rhythm and braced himself for hot spunk to gush down his throat.

Jonny, eyes closed, feeling a light breeze lick his forehead, suddenly heard a noise.

His eyes sprung open, needing to focus. "Damon…" He saw a red Toyota blocking the alleyway, as sensation began to rise and hurtle down his cock. Figures were climbing out, three men, one just in his teens. Another was large, formless, a sickly brute in Adidas. The third was skinny, face pitted with acne, a severe case of terminal ugliness. He stayed in the car at the driving wheel, glaring at Jonny with barely disguised disgust.

"Damon… stop." Jonny's heart juddered like a steamtrain. His words dug their heels into his throat and got no further. Just at that moment, his spunk pumped out into Damon's mouth. Damon swallowed, staring up at Jonny with an insane grin, his tongue glistening white. He rocked on his heels unaware of the figure advancing behind them. Jonny's cock lolled helplessly. His mind blitzed, seeing stars. He pulled ineffectually at Damon's collar.

In that instant, Damon sensed they had company. "Jonny…?" The back of his neck prickled. As he made to turn around there was a flurry of movement over his head that seemed to split the air asunder. Red spattered Damon's face. It felt warm on his cheeks. He scrambled backwards across the cobbles, staring in disbelief at Jonny who shuffled forward groggily, clutching a crimson stain that spread across his chest beneath the palm of his hand. Thick drops of blood oozed between Jonny's fingers. He swayed, seeking out Damon in the gloom where he still cowered on the ground in trauma. "Run. Fucking run…" whispered Jonny weakly, before stepping back punch drunk. He seemed to try to smile, but shadows greedily pulled him into the dark.

"Jonny!" Damon struggled to his feet, turning to face their assailants. He was confronted by excited faces, fucked-up and bold with bloodlust. The big fella advanced towards Damon; in his hand he wielded a serrated blade, laced crimson with Jonny's memory.

Damon didn't move, seeking out Jonny amongst the gloom of the alleyway. He thought he saw his body stir on the ground, accompanied by a soft moan. He began to edge slowly in that direction, considering darting forward, grabbing Jonny somehow and getting him out of there. It was completely insane, he knew – but Damon couldn't just leave him there.

The teenager, his gaze ping-ponging between his accomplice and Damon, allowed a cruel smile to creep onto his lips. He moved in to block Damon's access to Jonny, feeling his heels crunch onto limp fingers that didn't resist their weight.

"Let's get the fuck out of here!" The spotty lad revved the car impatiently. Damon saw shock-horror etched onto his face as he began to babble. "Oh God… oh God…"

The one holding the knife shook his head. "I haven't finished yet. C'mere fag," he snarled. "You like sucking cock?" He pulled at the elastic of his tracksuit bottoms and dug out his penis, rapidly filling with blood. "Suck on this then." Damon saw his belly heave excitedly, pale and immense in the moonlight.

The teenager laughed hard on a gobful of phlegm. "Eh, you fookin' poofter!"

The big fella snapped his trouser elastic back over his engorged prick. He spun around, not seeing the joke. "You calling me a queer?" The teenager's grin evaporated as the knife wavered dangerously close to his cheek. "No mate, only joking." He indicated Damon. "Let's just finish off the bender and get out of here."

"Come on!" screeched the driver from behind them.

The big fella nodded slowly and turned towards Damon, who was backtracking rapidly. He lunged forward and Damon darted between them all as the knife sliced the air. He cannoned into a dustbin, stinking of a week's unemptied trash, slipping on the soggy debris that spilled onto the ground. Damon cried out in frustration, choking on the taste of Jonny at the back of his throat.

"Get the fucker!" yelled the teenager, clambering over the avalanche of rubbish and plastic containers that rolled towards him. He picked up an empty wine bottle and smashed it against the wall. "Jesus, what a fuckin' stink!" Rank wafts of rotting meat choked the air.

Damon scrabbled up onto his feet, discarded tin can lids slicing into his hands as he struggled to keep upright. The knife cut down at his feet as the big fella struck out clumsily, also losing his balance as he stepped in the oozing mush. Damon dodged the blade and began to flee down the alley, the man with the knife hot on his tail. The driver watched goggle-eyed as Damon evaded their attempts to catch him, and fought with the car gears in white hot panic. The teenager jabbed a finger at him. "Go round the block and try to head him off!" He ran off after Damon.

The alley curled round the terraced garage lots into the sulphurous gleam of bright-lit Percy Street. Damon emerged into the open puffing like a locomotive, disorientated, ripped up inside. His hands dripped warm blood onto the paving stones, like a trail of sweets for the others to follow. He swivelled on his heels, caught in momentary indecision. What now? He looked around him at the imposing grey facades that offered no shelter – Liverpool slept, shutters closed. As he heard his attackers turn into the road, he blindly sprinted in one direction, running towards the jagged silhouette of Toxteth, bombed out against the fizzy orange sky. His face stung as if about to explode. Damon heard a cry behind him, a vengeful howl that would awaken the dead. It tickled the back of his neck where Jonny's fingers had strayed only minutes before. Jonny. Is he…? Please God, no!

Damon dashed straight into the road, blind to the red Toyota bearing right for him, foot on the accelerator. He glanced off the bonnet in a split-second mash of flesh and metal. Propelled by the collision, Damon's body was flung across the road like a ragdoll. He landed – badly – on his left collarbone, which he felt snap and sink into his chest. His head smacked onto the tarmac, sending his consciousness spinning. He considered blacking out as intense pain lashed his entire body. Easier to melt into the road and sleep. Jonny would come and save him, for sure…

But something caught Damon's attention in the corner of his eye. A sliver of soft light caressed him from an open front door, across the road. Despite his stupor, Damon felt sure he knew the figure beckoning frantically to him from the threshold. He pulled himself up from the ground. The left side of his face seemed reluctant to stay together and dripped onto his feet. At least it didn't hurt – in fact, no part of his body seemed to hurt now as a reassuring warmth enveloped him. He was vaguely aware of movement behind – figures scurrying towards him, a motor car turning in wrong gear, but he chose to ignore this, instead concentrating on the fuzzy figure that he instinctively knew represented safety. A hand, swathed in a pink crinoline dressing gown, reached out and grabbed his arm. Damon smelt hot cocoa and Chanel No.5, besides the pungent odour of gasoline and spilt blood.

"Jonny…"

"He's not here, love. Inside, quick."

"Charlene?"

"I'm here. Oh look what they've done to you."

"But Jonny. My Jonny."

Damon staggered over the threshold and blinked. Shards of 100 watt light daggered his bloodshot eyes; thick pile carpets sucked at his feet; furnishings baby blue and pink whirled in sickly confection. Sensory overload. His legs crumbled. Damon cracked reality-wise and succumbed, in relief, to the dark that danced behind his eyes. He was about to call it a day when, through the billowing shadows that buttressed his inner city, he saw Jonny. There he was! Right as rain. Grinning broadly at Damon, looking good, hair combed left-hand parting. His cheeks rosy, his grey-green eyes sparkling. Jonny called out to Damon, though for some reason the sound didn't carry. The boy seemed to have a lot to say. Damon reached out a hand, and Jonny likewise, till they touched pinkies but the darkness snapped at their fingers with black jaws, prising them apart. Something locked between them, invisible but impossible to breach. Damon struggled but couldn't prevent Jonny sinking into nowhere; the grin replaced by a look of consternation, his eyes seeking out Damon's own without success. Jonny was gone. Then Damon blacked out, feeling this immense, clammy sadness smother him.

10

A SLATE GREY SKY HUNG MONOLITHIC over the city towers and mossed suburban rank and file of identikit middle class rooftops. The humid air shivered sticky, scratching hot at buttoned shirt collars as husbands, wives, the gay and straight, went to work. A bitch of a day – not meant for niceties. Buses growled and belched sulphurous fumes that clung to the pockmarked hordes, dismal in taxi queues, wolfing down McDonald's burgers for breakfast. Cars buzzed angrily across clogged traffic junctions. Cigarette smoke congealed in the sweaty soup. Only the black shimmer of flying ants puckered the sobriety, in your hair, infesting.

The interlace of Georgian avenues behind town normally withstood the urban virus with equanimity, channelling its poisons into the heart of Toxteth. But today the ozone restricted the purifying flow; aggression hissed through cracked paving stones; bloody fantasies slithered amongst the undergrowth.

The news of Jonny's death spread, insidious, as the ambulance loaded his body. The hapless passer-by who had stumbled across the inert corpse fidgeted nervously while he clutched tight the lead of his excited Pit Bull. The tang of bloody confrontation, clinging to the crime scene like stubborn oil stains, sent the steel-coiled animal into catharsis.

A teenage policeman in uprolled shirtsleeves and come-to-bed eyes took notes as the Pit Bull sized him up malevolently. It growled at every sharp movement he made.

"So you say your dog led you to the body which was semi-concealed behind that skip?"

"That's right." The man cleared his throat nervously as people began to circulate, curious, as two forensics experts bent down over a rouge smear on the ground. Marker posts were dug into the grit; traces of violent activity highlighted in luminescence; a thick web of police activity smothering the starkness of spilt blood.

"And could you describe the body of the victim as you discovered it?"

"Him. He was a boy. A dead boy."

The policeman looked up, chastened, and the Pit Bull snapped an inch from his ankle. "Sorry sir. Him."

"Er… He'd lost a lot of blood, down his chest. It had dripped onto the ground, too. One shoe was a few feet away. That's what my dog saw first. He made a bit of a mess of that – I'm sorry. He has a thing about shoes, y'see…"

The policeman waved dismissively. "Don't worry about that, sir. Just tell me everything you can remember."

The man wiped his brow on his sleeve. "I think you know the rest. It looked to me like he'd been dragged across the ground, though someone tried to hide the tracks and all the blood…"

The Pit Bull sniffed at the fading crimson trail and caught a different scent muscling in. It cocked its head to one side and whimpered uncertainly, tapping a perplexed coda on the ground with its fat paws. A tall figure was pushing its way through the massing crowd, immaculate in dark Chanel suit, Gucci heels and a cloud of No.5. The Pit Bull's owner looked up in alarm at this dark vision, jet hair cascading onto large breasts barely held in check beneath a crisp, white shirt. The mutt cowered behind the policeman's ankles as he lowered his notepad to address the immaculately shaded face with a tight, burnished smile.

"Officer." The Amazonian proffered an elegant hand with slim fingers and cobalt-blue nail enamel. "My name is Charlene Monroe. Could you please tell me what has been happening here?"

144

The police officer craned his neck upward to take in this apparition looming before him. Overwhelmingly female in the fuck-me pout and the fuck-you stance, yet he sensed something savage – dare he say masculine – behind her aura.

"Can I ask you… miss, if you have any connection to this incident?" The policeman shuffled awkwardly as he was given a hard stare.

"*Ms,* if you don't mind," she snorted. "I believe I may have been a witness to whatever all this is about." She flicked her hair in the direction of the ambulance. "Can I just see whatever is *in there?*" She placed a clipped emphasis on the end of her sentences which leant authority to her to-the-pointness; so much so that, while questioning himself as to the unorthodox nature of his actions, the copper found himself, mesmerised, leading her to the ambulance.

"Be careful ms. It's not a pretty sight."

Charlene pulled herself into the van, hunching her backbone to squeeze her massive head of hair inside. The corpse's attendants withdrew sharpish as she grimly approached, pressing themselves against the sides of the ambulance.

Charlene stood over the covered body, hesitating to pull back the sheet. It was rare that she lost her nerve, but this was one of those occasions. Her manicured nails lingered over the starched cotton until she could stand it no longer. She lifted the cloth hurriedly.

"Oh my Lord," she gasped, clasping a delicate, tapering hand to her throat. Charlene replaced the sheet back over Jonny's head, stifling the smile that threatened to break out on her face. She had expected Serge but here, cold and pale, lay Jonny. The boy's face hardly betrayed the tragedy of the previous night, save a small cut on the forehead and traces of dirt wisping across his cheeks. Larger, darker bloodpools snaked up his neckline from beneath his corduroy shirt. On the contrary, he was a pretty sight. Jonny had never looked as pretty as he did now, with his ragged serenity and ice cream pallor. Charlene kissed his forehead, before placing the sheet back over his head.

She stepped away. "I've seen enough." Her Serge was still out there somewhere. He might be hiding from her, but she would catch up with him.

"This boy's name is Jonny James," she said flatly. "He was attacked last night on his way home, along with another boy, Damon Apostolidis, who I took, unconscious, to the Royal Liverpool Hospital last night. He was talking about Jonny before he lost consciousness. I assumed he was delirious, but they were obviously together when this happened."

Charlene wavered on her feet and the policeman reached over to support her. "Steady now, take it easy." He motioned to the ambulance attendants to help him lift Charlene out of the ambulance. It took two of them to do it effectively.

"I'm sorry you had to go through that Ms Monroe," continued the policeman calmly, completely charmed by her despite himself. "However, it is imperative that you tell me what you saw last night." He pulled out his notepad from his top pocket.

She gracefully acknowledged the attentiveness of the ambulance attendants. "Thank you gentlemen, I'm fine now." She paused, her face set with concentration. "I don't know," she faltered, "it was all a blur. Over so quickly." She looked ready to burst into tears. "Oh, I'm no good at this!"

"Just try and remember," said the policeman gently.

Charlene took a deep breath. "I was stirring myself my bedtime cocoa, about 4.30am, I think, when I heard all this commotion in the street. I pulled back the curtains and I saw my Damon staggering about in the middle of the road. He looked in a bad way, blood all down his face. Those poor boys!" She hid her face in her hands.

"You're doing fine, Ms Monroe," coaxed the policeman. "And then what did you see?"

"I saw three men, I think, two running towards Damon, another in an old car. The noise I heard was the car – it must have just hit Damon. I didn't think about anything but getting my boy out of there, they were all running towards him. I rushed out and managed to get Damon into my flat before they could lay another finger on him."

"Very good, I'm proud of you," smiled the policeman reassuringly. "Now, think hard. Can you remember what any of these men looked like?"

Charlene frowned, looking agonised. "Oh it's hopeless!" she cried. "I'm not sure. I will have to think about it. All I was interested in was in Damon's safety." She stared mournfully at the policeman.

He cursed silently. "Alright ms. Don't worry. We'll come back to that. Can you identify the vehicle the one man was driving?"

"I… think it was red."

This was hardly enough to build an investigation on. "OK," said the copper slowly, becoming dispirited that this lady was such a poor witness, "did you see the deceased at all at this time?"

Charlene shook her head.

"Any idea what could be the motive behind the incident?"

Charlene again shook her head silently.

The policeman felt it was time to restore this lady's faith in law and order. "Ms. Monroe," he said, "I'm sorry, really sorry. We in the force are giving our all to prevent incidents like this ever happening. You can be sure we'll be onto these bastards as soon as we get a lead. But we will need your co-operation, as soon as you remember something – *anything*. You may be vital to the resolution of this crime."

He was surprised by Charlene running her fingers through his soft hair. She was smiling now, beautiful, tragedy held in check. "Sure hon. What's your name?"

He was disarmed by her intimacy. "Billy, miss. Ms."

"And how old are you, Billy?"

"Nineteen."

Charlene sighed, world-weary. "So much responsibility when so young, Billy." She wet a finger and flattened unruly hairs on his right eyebrow. "You might find that some people aren't prepared to wait for the police to catch up with them." She took a business card from her breast pocket and placed it in Billy's warm palm. He examined it in bemusement: 'Charlene Monroe – entrepreneur'. "You have my full co-operation, son. These kids were friends of mine. My babies. Someone has got it in for them. If you find out anything yourself, I'd appreciate it if you returned the favour. My number's on the card."

Charlene turned on her heels and went over to talk to Billy's superior officer who had just, at that moment, arrived on the scene. Superintendent Ivanosec and Ms Monroe seemed to know each other pretty well, Billy thought. He wandered back to the alleyway where the boy had been murdered. The forensics work was done; ticker tape cordoned off the area completely and a policeman stood impassive over the small crowd of onlookers.

Billy wondered what was the story with Ms Monroe. There was something to her that eluded his perception. Nonetheless, he had to grab swiftly at his crotch to relieve the erection pushing at his stay-pressed. He looked around furtively to confirm that his cock went unnoticed.

A detective came over and produced a clear transparent bag, dangling it before Billy's gaze. Inside was a tatty ticket stub from the Curzon. "Found this on the deceased."

Billy frowned, peering at the scrap of paper. "What is it?"

"An entrance receipt for one of those fag bars. Dated last night." He sniffed. "Look's like another queer bites the dust. Can't say I'm too sorry."

Billy blanched. "Just show it to the Superintendent, alright?" Billy was well aware how some of his workmates in the force felt about poofters, but he didn't let himself get involved with their fucked-up attitude. Live and let live, he thought. What harm did they do – as long as they didn't lay a finger on him there was nothing to worry about from his point of view, was there? If they bought him a beer they were a friend for life.

In the locker room at the station you couldn't turn your back, otherwise some joker would be rubbing himself semi-hard against your arse while mouthing off about faggots. Billy knew that on E these lads might, for the crack, end up at Garlands amongst all these screaming queens in DKNY vests. But after a pissed up night down the local they might just as quickly be in the mood for leaving some queer for dead down a dark alley.

Billy wondered if some of his workmates were capable of murder.

He fingered the card in his pocket that reeked of No.5.

Jonny James got to be in the papers. It started local, there he was front page – "Red's hopeful tragic death," "Murder victim of gay attack." Photo-immortalised with a twinkle in his eye and a boy band grin. In the daily glut of lurid non-news, the nationals picked up the story, and even a few TV crews fished around for an angle. He was brutally murdered, sexy *and* gay; a tidal wave in the rock pool of human disinterest. How can you protect your gay child, asked Richard and Judy? Why homos should stay in the closet, ranted *The Daily Mail*.

All that was rotten in the state of England found its nemesis in Jonny James. At the putrid heart of this peculiar animal, the high priests of tabloid preached their hyperactive creed of moral rectitude with a sly nod to their sponsors. Who were these shadowy figures wielding their opinions like blunt instruments, beating the public into submission? In this artificial hothouse where anyone and everyone were fair game, how did these paper puppeteers themselves stay so stubbornly out of the media spotlight?

For decades the dailies had nurtured a climate of reactionary homophobia fuelled on stunted patriotism and mad-cow ignorance. The subtle shift of sympathies post-Jonny smacked of opportunism, a canny appraisal of the yin and yang of the public mood. After a decade of disco cross-fertilisation, enough heterosexuals had realised that queers weren't Satan's little helpers but, in fact, they were coming out in a family near you. Your cousin was a lesbian, your little nephew was out, your dad was divorced and shacking up with the man next door...

Television, 'drag' of a nation, wore its authenticity on its silicon chest with pride. It clamped onto intimate human tragedy like a leech, smoothing the rough edges and reducing it to bite-size telenuggets. Satellite prowled around the outskirts, nipping at BBC heels with an animalistic hunger for broad strokes. Mrs James's nervous breakdown sent her cachet Sky-high. No more money worries now. There were Jonny's parents on *Good Morning* television, hosed down and clipped, uncomprehending and bathetic. Your story shames us all, cooed the sycophantic television presenter amidst the pastel furnishings which they drooled over in quiet awe. Mrs James regarded the interviewer's big hair and saw opportunity and ambitious perms. Her husband even managed to crack a joke by the end of the transmission and the camera crew rose to its feet, applauding Scouse courage in the face of adversity.

Amongst this mass exorcism of a nation's guilt complexes, Jonny blurred and became curiously asexual. The media abstracted and ultimately cancelled him out, till the sacrifice of this gay boy meant nothing but a chaste soundbite. The gay community, hopeful for its 15 minutes of fame, was left dressed up with nowhere to go. Fifth form girls and checkout opportunists called Trisha had their say, yet, in his hospital bed Damon wasn't news.

Liverpool 8 scowled and fed on its frustrations. D for Demo day rapidly took on a greater significance as Jonny's killers remained at large, despite the crude photofit faces glaring down from lamp posts and brick walls. Toxteth bided its time behind closed doors. The police force tied itself in knots.

From first light a large crowd converged on Huskisson Street, bussed in from the grey suburbs, even Manchester. Disco bunnies straight from Paradise Factory; M & S housewives; on-the-dolers from Everton. A convoy of sixties sports cars pulled up at the crowd edge, an Aston Martin leading the way. From the driver's seat a smartly-dressed, peak-capped chauffeur climbed out to hold open the passenger door; Charlene emerged, a little ungainly. She was becoming too big for her choice of vehicle. In the Carmen Ghia behind sat Madame Lafayette and Miss Golightly, staring impassively at the mass of people that ogled them curiously. A young child stepped a little too close, reaching out in barely-disguised wonder while pulling on his mummy's hand – Miss Golightly hissed at him like a wildcat. The boy's mother yanked him back hurriedly.

Charlene looked around satisfactorily at the numbers present for this, her first show of strength. It felt good to be back. Self-confidence fizzed in her veins. She motioned to Madame Lafayette to remain in her car and likewise the other transsexuals that brooded from the security of their vehicles, some looking slightly haggard this early in the morning. But as Charlene told them: world domination was not for late risers.

"Serge!" Charlene waved frantically as she saw him emerge through the bustle, holding onto Katy Ann. Sharma followed, chatting with her next door neighbour, a computer hacker named Jo. Charlene had wanted an introduction to this fearless dyke for some time, but it would have to wait – there was more pressing business to attend to.

All looked up at Charlene as she scurried over. "Well, what have you got to say for yourself? I've been worried sick."

Serge grimaced sheepishly. "I've nothing to say."

Charlene flicked back her hair. "But where are you staying? I've been looking everywhere for you."

"You haven't been looking very hard then. Sharma said I could stay with her." He looked gratefully at her.

"Oh. I see." Charlene put her hands on her hips and glared sternly at Serge, coiled tight. A second passed and she lunged forward in an electrifying arc, grabbing at Sharma's hair and pulling hard, wrapping the long locks around her fist. The girl yelped, scrabbling at her lustrous black mane. "So you've stolen my boy from me – homebreaker! Trollop!" Sharma flailed out at the transsexual's face but Charlene avoided her wild swings, tugging harder on the girl's hair. Sharma screeched louder. "Get off me!" Katy Ann went to launch herself at Charlene but Serge held her back, while pulling at the transsexual's iron grip. Eventually Charlene let go, snarling; she came away with a fistful of black hair.

Sharma stepped back hurriedly, face bright red. Serge cut in. "That's enough! Think of Jonny! What way is this to honour his memory?" Serge moved between them and jutted his chin out defiantly. "Actually Charlene, it was me who went to Sharma."

"You?" she said, dumbfounded. "But – why? What have I done? Surely we could have worked this one out baby?" The hefty transsexual looked crushed, for once at a loss for words.

Serge was aware of all eyes on him as he confronted his mentor. "Well," he began slowly, sensing the words spill from his mouth without any consideration of their content, "I thought you wanted to help me, but all you are is – a control freak. You never cared for my feelings. I want to be with people who really care for me. You – you're like Slobodan Milosevic, but in drag." Serge looked at Charlene imperiously. "And even *he* would look better in Chanel."

Charlene gasped, aware of the colour draining from her cheeks. Distracted by the spectacle, a group of passers-by observed fascinated, thinking the fun had already commenced. Charlene's lower lip trembled as she struggled to regain her composure. Realising her posture was a disgrace, she straightened her back. She blew her fringe from her eyes and puffed her chest out proudly. "If that's the way you see it, then Sharma is welcome to you. You make a lovely couple. So sweet." She looked around, then consulted her watch. "This matter is concluded. It's time for action." She slipped away, uncharacteristically discrete.

Serge looked at Sharma in concern. "You alright?" He kissed her forehead tenderly.

Sharma nodded. "I'm OK."

"That bloody bitch!" continued Serge bitterly.

"Let's just forget it," interrupted Sharma firmly. "As you reminded us, we're here for Jonny's sake and nothing else."

Serge nodded slowly. "Yeah." He looked around. "Look at all these people here. All for our Jonny. If only Damon could see this." He pointed over Sharma's shoulder. "Maybe he will. Look – TV."

Sharma nodded as they watched a film crew setting up their equipment at a safe distance. "They're not taking any chances," she said.

"Are we gonna be on TV mam?" asked Katy Ann, tugging at her mother's leg.

"Yes, love. So I don't want you showing off. Nan and grandad will probably be watching."

"Ace!"

Sharma bent down to her daughter's level. "You still want to do it like we said? You're not too angry at Charlene or your mam?"

Katy Ann nodded. "This is for Jonny. And we know Charlene really is another horrible man, 'cept in drag."

Serge tapped Sharma on the shoulder. "Here's Gus."

"Hiya," Gus joined them, rubbing the sleep out of his eye.

"Another late night?" asked Serge pointedly.

"No. I couldn't sleep at all, actually." Gus looked hurt. "Are you ready then? It's coming up to time. Damon's mum will be along in a moment with the wreath." He shook his head sadly. "She's in a right state."

"I bet," said Serge. He took a deep breath. "Alright then? You first."

Gus found Charlene, who stood at one side silently watching. They conferred briefly and Gus moved to the head of the excited mass of people. Serge, Sharma and Katy Ann joined him, power dressed in stark solidarity; Gus had painted his fingernails black jet. Placards swayed above the bobbing heads – "Zero Tolerance for the Intolerant," "Justice for Jonny," "This Witch is not for Burning!" Flashbulbs flared and hissed from the outer limits of the psyched-up throng – journalists tempted back to the story by the threat of further confrontation.

The mass of protesters came to rest before the tenement terrace that housed the unsuspecting Scallies who had threatened Gus and Serge two weeks before. Ocean Colour Scene filtered through an open window into the street. Gus's pink graffiti masterwork still glittered on the white wall. Below it had been hurriedly scribbled, "Kill the bumboys."

A tense hush descended.

"Go on now, love." Sharma bent down to Katy Ann, giving her a reassuring grin.

"Affirmative." In her arms Katy Ann held a wreath of black silk flowers. She looked up at her circle of friends and jutted out her chin in elegant determination. "For Jonny."

She went up to the front door and rang the bell four times in quick succession. Scant moments passed before a tousle-haired youth came to the door in a *Loaded* T-shirt and panda bear boxers. He took in the curious sight of this ten year old little girl in black leather. "What's this about?" he muttered irritably before noticing the crowd swelling behind her. His eyes bulged out of their sockets at the silent multitude stretched out across the length of Huskisson Street. "What the fuck…?"

Katy Ann brandished the wreath under his nose, barely disguising the loathing in her pretty cocoa face. "This is to remember Jonny by, who you killed with your hate."

The Scally stared incredulously at her as the first rotten fruit flew over his head and spattered on the stairwell. He ducked and quickly shut the front door before a showerstorm of debris clattered onto the peeling enamel. Katy Ann was scooped up into her mother's arms as the mass surged forward and bounced off the front door, carried by its own momentum. Gus and Serge were there, ramming the door open beside a host of lesbians from the Wirral that bashed the splintering wood with mallets and crowbars. A brick cut the air and split a window pane asunder, showering them with glass. They brushed aside the sharp fragments and carried on. The crowd cheered, spitting out slogans – "No More Mr Nice Gay!" "Fear the Queer! Fear the Queer!" It were as though a lifetime's frustrations were being exorcised on this tarmac and formica battlefield – for sniggers and snide remarks, for prejudice in the workplace, for parental put-downs, for knife to the throat tragedies. The sludgy ozone smelt nasty and, from afar, the familiar howl of Mersey Police sirens added to the cacophony. The whole building seemed to shake with their rage, until they broke through the front door, ripping it off its hinges. A roar of blood-curdling intensity went up from the crowd, lashing the dirty sky, as half a dozen lesbians and gays plunged into the hallway and up the stairs.

"This one!" yelled Gus excitedly, stopping before a tatty door with bags of rubbish dumped on the landing. "Clear!" ordered one of the lesbians, who immediately began hacking away at the lock with an axe. Serge raised his eyebrows and grinned at Gus, who winked back. They kissed each other impulsively. "Through!" The dyke kicked open the shattered door with her boot and stepped into the flat, Gus and Serge immediately behind her. "There goes one!" she yelled. Her mates piled after the lad who tried to shut himself in the bathroom, screaming hysterically. He pushed against the door in desperation but the lesbians were far stronger and fell through onto him, his head cracking against the sink.

Gus and Serge scoured the flat for the other lad, smashing up belongings as they went along. They tipped the stereo and television onto the floor, shattering the Plexiglas finish. Serge threw a pile of CDs out the window in disgust: Led Zeppelin; Sting; Pink Floyd; Kula Shaker. "Crap, crap and more crap. I want Boyzone! I want Kylie!" he pronounced. "The bastard's hiding!" said Gus frustratedly. Serge nodded. At that moment he saw someone slip out of the front door. "There he goes!" he shouted. They raced after him and lunged at his feet as the lad dived horizontally. The three tumbled over each other, landing in an untidy heap halfway down. Serge immediately began punching the man in the face while Gus extricated himself, dazed, from underneath and then woozily began to put the boot in.

Down in the street, the missiles continually bombarded the facade. From somewhere in the crowd a Molotov cocktail soared skywards and plopped gracefully through the broken window. An "oooh" escaped from the mesmerised demonstrators before there was a woomph of energised O_2. A tiger yellow fireball cannonballed into space and sent shards of glass and masonry into the crowd. People screamed and scattered in blind panic. Through the splintered front door Gus and Serge hurtled out into the street, faces black with soot, along with the lesbians bellowing triumphantly. A cloud of grey smoke followed them. Not far behind were the two Scally lads, driven out from their lair. They were immediately ambushed by a crowd of expectant queers who punched and kicked them to the floor, before hoisting them into the air roughly. One sported a bloody nose and sobbed, "Leave me alone, please! We didn't do anything! Don't hurt me!" His protests fell on the deaf ears of the frenzied mob hungry for blood.

Three patrol cars turned simultaneously into Huskisson Street, sirens blazing. They skidded to a halt at the amorphous crowd edge, swerving to avoid the unexpected convoy of smart sports cars that roared noisily away from the riot scene. People skidded in all directions, hurtling over the glossy bonnets of the police vehicles in a surreal steeplechase, as officers scrabbled to catch the fleeing figures. The Scally lads were left in a crumpled heap on the bloodstained pavement, one slack-jawed, probably broken. The other seeped goo from his nose and cranium, jerking spasmodically. One protestor aimed a final kick at his face and was brought down by the nimblest of coppers who shackled him to some railings before going off in pursuit of a leatherclad biker dyke. Others chased the gay, lesbian and sympathetic that retreated from the riot scene; one handcuffed a bony pensioner securing a snappy Chihuahua. Journalistic hacks snapped maniacally with their telephoto lenses, stunned by the insane choreography.

Smoke belched from the third floor, spitting orange sparks. The downstairs neighbour nervously opened the window and poked her head into the street, surveying the scene of destruction. She hadn't seen anything like this since the Blitz. A hole in her ceiling showered dust and duckdown onto her living room floor.

The police, red faced and adrenalised, were swift in their retribution, herding stragglers together like cattle for the slaughter. Stray faggots, shiny faced and euphoric, still clenched their fists in the air and shouted gay rights slogans, but, by now, the coppers had things under control. One biffed a particularly noisy boy. "Shut it sonny!" He was shot a venomous glance and the boy shouted, "Police brutality – innocent mortality!" "Yeah yeah," sighed the policeman wearily.

The remaining few were soon handcuffed and catapulted into a police van. As the air settled and the twitching bodies of the Scallies were shovelled up off the pavement, fire engines could be heard clattering to the scene.

Journalists finished off their rolls of film with shots of uprooted shrubbery, broken glass rivers and smears of orange blood. The television crew gave their post mortem and cut.

The neighbourhood poked its nose out cautiously, wondering what had hit them. Liverpool swept yet more of its casualties under the carpet of indifference.

A Metropolitan Police helicopter swooped over the battleground, whirring noisily, but its incessant drone passed unnoticed. The populace was used to its presence whenever it tracked down escaped convicts or joy riders on the city horizon. The chopper passed through a noxious cloud of polyurethane cinders rising high above the Liverpool rooftops, and the Protestant cathedral's imposing thrust into the sky, casting a dank green shimmer onto the Mersey's soft belly.

The hospital ward was long and low, north-facing, shrouding the patients in permanent shadow. In spite of this the heavy Venetian blinds were pulled down, permitting only wafer-thin slivers of light to penetrate. They strafed the patients like razor blades.

Someone had switched on the luminescent strip lighting to dispel the gloom, yet it had the opposite effect; it only served to contrast the brilliant day outside with the dankness within.

Nurses in pleats sent dust particles billowing as they stripped a recently-vacated bed of its soiled sheets. Their excited babble about treacherous boyfriends and phantom pregnancies prickled the sickroom hush like hecklers at a funeral.

"So we're down the pub having a pint and the slag comes over and gives my Dave a kiss."

"No…"

"So I says, 'Get yer tits out me boyfriend's face, you.' And she says, 'I was gonna say the same thing to you, you fat cow!' "

"No…"

"So I says to Dave, 'What's she mean by that, eh? You're not gonna let her get away with that, are you?' And he says, 'Oh, fuck off the pair of yous,' and goes off and sits with that bitch Louise."

"No…"

The patients sat and stewed, hemmed in by starched bed linen. The impassive, whiskered faces of the old and infirm blanked out their sepulchral surroundings, propped up against the head board to keep death at bay.

One bald-pated sextagenarian with white fluffy earlobes ground his teeth incessantly, his chin whirring like an express train. Another jerked forward in a clockwork effort to pull himself out of bed, his legs, nevertheless, remaining resolutely immobile. He could not have been older than 45.

The air smelt of mothballs and antiseptic, piqued by Matron's sulphurous Avon fragrance. Gus gagged on the acrid cocktail, clutching onto Katy Ann's hand for comfort as they approached the bed at the end of the ward. Serge and Sharma followed in silence. Damon lay there, collar bone swathed in gauze, a patch over one eye. He noticed their cautious approach and jumped, pulling his legs up to his chest.

The visitors forced a smile, attempting to reassure the boy, wretched in his NHS bed. Katy Ann spontaneously leapt into Damon's lap and he softened, though he winced in unwelcome pain.

"Katy Ann, geroff o' there love." Sharma darted forward to pull the little girl off the bed.

"No no," said Damon, "it's alright." He ruffled Katy Ann's hair. "Hiya Jubilee. What happened in the *X-Men* this week, then?"

Katy Ann looked around disapprovingly. "Can't you watch the *X-Men* here?"

Damon shook his head. "All I get to see is *Grandstand* and *Surprise Surprise.*" He cast a look around morosely. "It's the company I keep these days."

Serge pointed to the big bouquet of pink orchids that shimmered by the bedside. "I see that we are not here first."

"Charlene," said Damon. "She brought mail and me Game Boy. Gave me all the news." He cast his eyes down to the floor. They could all see tight anger pulse in his drawn cheeks. "Charlene told me *everything.*"

Sharma mumbled awkwardly, "Damon, we don't know what to say…"

"Save it. You're not gonna make things any better by feeling sorry for me. Jonny's dead and nothing's gonna bring him back." Damon's voice rose a decibel and disturbed the nurses, who looked daggers at him. The other patients resolutely ignored his outburst.

Gus squirmed in his DMs. This was all his fault. Because of his amateur hour delusions of grandeur, a bright, innocent boy in love with a world that loved him back was rotting in the morgue. He found himself shaking like a leaf as he babbled, "We showed 'em, Damon! We gave 'em hell the other day. You would have been proud. It got in the papers and everything."

Damon grimaced. "Yeah smart, mate. I saw it on the box. You were all great." He confronted Gus with a steely gaze. "But it's not enough, is it? Jonny's dead. He's dead…" His voice trailed off.

"The police are looking for the suspects, Damon," added Sharma. "They've doubled their efforts since the demo. They've started to take us seriously at last."

Damon snorted derisively. "Charlene's got more of an idea than they have. She's busy nosing around Toxteth while the police are off down the pub. I've already got their names, thanks to her. They're just waiting for this to die down and then they'll be back out again, looking for someone else to knock about. The law can do fuck all about it."

Serge glanced over at Gus, who wavered in stricken torture. He mutely took Gus's hand in his own, caressing the open palm with his thumb. Gus looked at Serge, a lonestar tear burning his left cheek until it fizzed on his parched upper lip.

"Damon, you'll be out of here soon," said Serge. "We can get back to normal."

"Things will never be the same again, Serge." All were surprised by the icy vehemence in Damon's voice.

"We brought you some grapes," intervened Sharma hastily. She handed over a little brown paper bag. "Seedless."

"And some magazines, " added Gus, *"Sky, Elle* and *Vanity Fair."*

"Thanks." Damon smiled, a peculiar, empty contortion of his splintered face. "You know what I miss the most? How important he made me feel. Now he's gone, I dunno if I remember his face even. Funny, isn't it?" No one was laughing.

"Suddenly, me life meant something," he continued. "Giving me soul to another person." He winced as he sat up further in his bed. "Then, when that person is taken away from you you're left with such a fucking big hole, and something has to fill that hole. All I know is there's hate in me now, where Jonny used to be. I want to do to those cunts what they did to Jonny. I want them to fucking die…"

Sharma sat on the edge of the bed. "Jesus Damon, you're scaring me!"

Gus panicked. "Hasn't enough shit happened, for Chrissakes!" He looked wildly to Serge for support.

Serge motioned for calm aware that Charlene had been there spreading her poison. He felt heartily sick, wishing that she would leave them alone, once and for all. "Damon, what good would it do? It's over, you must see? You have to learn to deal with Jonny's death in other ways. Revenge just fucks things up more – you are giving them excuse for more violence. Don't forget, we're better than those bastards – a lot of people realise that now. We've got respect, finally."

"Respect?" laughed Damon. "That's what you call it? Some would say you gave straights a new excuse to avoid us like the plague. Have you seen the papers?"

Sharma spoke up quietly. "He's right. *The Echo's* calling it a disgrace, like it was anarchy or something. *The Sun's* demanding tough measures against gays, beefing up Clause 28 and all that, saying queers have got too big for their own boots."

Gus grimaced. "I bet Charlene's pissed off."

"You think so?" continued Sharma. "I think gay equality was the last thing on her mind. She's probably chuffed to have the bad publicity – it makes her look harder."

"Yeah, you're right," said Gus despondently, lowering his eyes.

"Look mates," said Damon, suddenly softer, "I'm tired. I need to rest if I stand any chance of getting out before Bert, next door, kicks the bucket."

Sharma looked across to the near lifeless husk wound up in tubes and drips. "I wouldn't fancy hanging round for that," she said wryly. "Yup, let's go! Katy Ann, off o'there."

Damon called for a glass of water. The ward nurse loomed behind them and announced that visiting time was over. They all looked at each other ominously.

Their goodbyes were awkward, inarticulate. Damon returned their hugs and kisses but ill concealed the malaise that clung tenaciously to his brow. Gus tried to tally this Damon with the boy he first met in Jody's three years before: soul mate, partner in petty crime and big-hearted chump. Now Gus saw a complete stranger before him. Damon had lived a lifetime in the intensity of weeks – he was out of Gus's league. It scared him. "Look after yourself, babe," he said. But it rang hollow, echoing in the fusty air.

They left the ward in mute silence, chilled to the bone by the sight of these old men preserved in formaldehyde in their starched beds, unvisited, unwanted. Poky eyes squinted accusingly after them as they quickened their pace. "Jesus Christ," muttered Sharma, "I think I'll top meself before I end up in one of those places. I feel guilty for breathing." Katy Ann pulled at her hand, eager to get away. Sharma let go and she skipped ahead, relieved to get out into the oily urban air and play with her DC fantasies.

Gus opened the door to his top floor Canning Street bedsit and ushered Serge inside. He motioned Serge to sit on the sixties Italian sofa he had bought, dirt cheap, at a Huyton car boot sale. "So, you want coffee?" Gus sounded weary and depressed. Serge nodded mutely.

Gus went off to the kitchenette which was concealed behind a bamboo curtain that chinked in the swirling air. The sun descended over the Mersey and the city jumble, throwing a purple shadow.

Serge cast his eyes around, his gaze lingering on the poster of Richey Edwards from the Manic Street Preachers. The slight, bruised face stared out from the wall, dark rings under bloodshot eyes. Gus had always said how much he identified with the stricken pop star. His disappearance had disturbed the boy deeply, yet Serge sensed that Gus found the tragic mystique almost sexy. He ran his fingers along the mantelpiece where Gus's precious collection of Richard Allen paperbacks was arranged. Two Italian marble bookends, from Pearl in San Diego, held the well-thumbed pulp in check. Serge looked at his fingers that came away grey, thick with dust. "Can I put on a CD?" he hollered, anxious to dispel the funereal air.

"Go ahead."

Serge smiled to himself as he pulled a little Virgin Megastore bag from his pocket, inserting a CD into the hi-fi. Toni Braxton boomed from the speakers. Gus emerged with two mugs of steaming Nescafé. He frowned. "This CD isn't mine."

"It is now. Prezzie."

Gus placed a mug into Serge's outstretched hand. "For me?"

"Don't be so surprised."

"Thanks." Gus supped noisily on the coffee froth. "I like it. Did you know this song's a bit rude?"

"I know, I've been here already." Gus opened his mouth to speak. "Don't ask," butted in Serge. He changed the subject. "So I'm finally to get the cup of coffee you promised me."

"Yeah…" answered Gus, smiling coyly. "But I'm still waiting for that dinner you promised me."

Serge nodded. "That's right." He cast his mind back, trying to recall quite why. He grimaced; they both realised simultaneously that Jonny's murder had spoilt their appetites. "I make up for it, don't you worry," Serge said quietly.

Gus sighed. "One good thing about this, I suppose. My parents wrote to me the other day. They got the fright of their lives imagining what might happen to their beloved son."

"That's great, Gus."

He shrugged his shoulders. "I guess." Gus felt strangely unmoved by their gesture. Characteristically, the letter had been mum's work with dad grudgingly roped in. Gus sensed his father's coolness behind the gushing facade, and was surprised at his own indifference. Maybe he had put that ghost to rest at last; he wasn't about to fail those who had supported him while his family had turned their back on him. "Serge, what do you think is going to happen to Damon?"

Serge put down his coffee cup. "I don't know. He seems pretty bad."

Gus sat back pensively. "I'm worried. Everyone thinks he's got his head screwed on right, but I've seen him when he's been low."

Serge nodded. "We had to watch him day and night, in case he did something stupid to himself." Serge pondered for a moment. "I don't know. He seems – different. Aggressive maybe."

"He gave me a fright, all this talk of revenge," agreed Gus.

They looked at each other, both trying to blot out the rush of pernicious foreboding that threatened to overwhelm them. Serge touched Gus's knee. "You OK?"

Gus smiled weakly. "Yeah." A lot had happened since their fight in Huskisson Street. Their own problems had taken a back seat; without even realising it they had grown close to each other. Their eyes met fleetingly. Could they also love each other?

"What about you?" asked Gus cautiously.

"Me? I'm alright." Serge found his throat drying up. "Why?"

"Oh well, you know, the last time we were together, alone like this, you were a bit – wound up."

Serge winced at the memory. "Good coffee," he said, putting the mug to his lips and glugging down a mouthful of bitter liquid.

"You don't have to tell me anything," ventured Gus bravely. "But I'm your mate and if I can help at all…"

Serge remembered making the same offer to Gus and having it thrown back in his face. "Yeah, my mate." Serge wasn't ready yet to open up with Gus, or with anyone. One day though, he might like Gus to be special enough for him to take that risk. He flexed his fingertips. "Gus, I was thinking…" He suddenly became lost for words. Gus was now staring at him fixedly. This was difficult. "Do you want to go out with me?" He went bright red and gulped down his coffee.

Gus looked at this big, muscled bear, with his dark-lashed eyes, Botticelli lips, ruffled hair and marble skin that never tanned. Serge looked for all the world like some stud from an eastern European porn flick, way out of Gus's league. He ran his fingers through the thick mop of tawny hair and, perhaps for the first time in his life, he felt truly certain of what he wanted. "Yeah," he said, "I want to go out with you."

Gus woke up suddenly, the familiar panic welling up in his confused mind. He turned in his creaky bed. Relieved, he saw Serge there, sleeping peacefully. One arm clutched the pillow while the other cradled his large cock. He looked good enough to eat.

Serge and Gus had eventually made love. Coyly, they had opened up to each other, exploring each other's bodies with the tender wonder of babies. They had climaxed in each other's arms, working their lover's cock, mouths clamped together in a sweet, intense kiss. They shook as their joint orgasm rippled across their bodies, lost in the dynamics of boy on boy.

Gus trailed his tongue across his parched lower lip. His throat felt woody; it had taken a full bottle of wine to overcome their inhibitions. He rose, padding to the kitchenette to pour himself a glass of water.

As he supped gratefully on his glass, he moved over to the bay window and peered blearily at the panoramic expanse of Liverpool that stretched below him. Home. Smoky chimney stacks and relics of seventies utopian follies. Dickensian warehouses in steady decay and vandal proof bus shelters. Greasy Chinatown neon billboards and the elegant contours of the Walker Art Gallery. Gus screwed up his eyes. Between the hulking block of St George's Hall and the Walker he could see the cold blue flicker of stationary police vehicles. Further squad cars hurtled across town towards the commotion, their sirens just audible. Had something happened at the Peace Gardens? Maybe a punch up involving late-night stragglers from the State. It wouldn't be the first time.

He washed out his glass and was on the point of climbing back under the bedcovers when the telephone rang. Annoyed, he glanced at the clock radio. 4.42am. Who the hell would be phoning at this hour? Moaning softly, Serge stirred by his side. Gus reached over him and picked up the receiver.

11

CHARLENE SAT AT HER DRESSING TABLE, astringent smears drying on her pale cheeks. The criss-cross of ageing emerged from beneath. She dabbed at her eyes with a soggy cotton wool swab, wincing under the weight of false lashes.

She paused and considered her tatty reflection. Time was a cruel bed partner she thought, as she pulled out her hair grips one by one. Wispy sheen-less locks slipped down, collecting in an inert bundle.

She checked her watch and cursed the time. 3.37am. Jesus Christ! No wonder she looked rough, if these were the hours she kept. Still, she couldn't resist the invitation from the Divine David to co-host the alternative talent contest for Manchester Mardi Gras. Fame and Channel 4 beckoned for the unquestionable winner, a lesbian ventriloquist with a Maggie Thatcher doll. Charlene noted the exquisite irony in having a hand up *that* skirt.

She supped at the lone glass of whiskey that was her constant lover and companion. She had given up on sexual kicks many moons ago. Her medication had recently begun to puff her up like a barrage balloon. Her shoulders were somehow stretching horizontally like an American football player's; her hips, clinging desperately to the emptiness between her legs, seemed to be widening like pastry under a rolling pin. Her hunger for femininity – precious, exquisite, fierce – knew no bounds. She would do anything to pass as a woman and, in fact, she had, defying biology, breaking the law and wiping out all who stood in her way. Yet sisterhood eluded her. Most women steered clear of her, uncomfortable with her strident plasticity. She felt a sham, a scientific anomaly, a Frankenstein's monster in expensive cosmetics and designer drag. Pretty soon the illusion would no longer succeed in hiding the joins. The world had better watch out when that day came.

Charlene picked up a brush and began pulling it through her hair, lost in moroseness. She had believed if Serge had been able to dig her then she could have glossed over her imperfections. But he was right – his rejection had showed her up for a spiteful old has-been.

Well fuck him.

Fuck them all.

Anger and frustration bit her ribs and, impulsively, she reached in her drawer for more cigarettes. Her hand came to rest on a black and white photo in an ornate antique silver frame. Frowning, Charlene made to conceal it again under the papers scattered across the drawer, but then reconsidered. Involuntarily, she sneaked a wary look over her shoulder before pulling out the photo frame.

She regarded the image stonily. "Ugh! Ugly little bastard, weren't you?" she commented drily. She saw a plain-looking young man sitting before the Pierhead on a windswept winter's day, seagulls swooping above his thick Brylcreemed hair. The face was sharply angular, eyes piggy and mean, glaring at the camera. The lips were pursed tight with unintentional femininity and his arms were folded.

Charlene blinked. She wondered why she had always resisted the temptation to throw the photograph away. Perhaps she worried that if she sacrificed this last testament to her past, then she would lose altogether her already tenuous grip on reality. This young man, Charlie Monroe at the beginning of a notorious underworld career, remained a stranger to her. Dockside orphan, pimp, pusher, prostitute – Charlene thought she had read about his life rather than lived it, perhaps in some Charles Dickens penny paperback.

She lit herself a Gaulois filched from a cheap weekend in Paris. It tasted foul. She returned the photograph to the drawer and carefully rearranged the papers over it.

Impassively, she picked up her hairbrush again and began to drag it through her auburn mane.

The phone rang, startling Charlene out of her reverie. She leant over and removing an earring, placed the receiver to her delicate ear. "Hullo?" Her voice sounded like stones poured into a metal bucket.

There was a pause before the caller spoke up, furtively, in guttural whispers. Charlene recognised his voice from somewhere; a soft, adolescent burr.

"Ms… Monroe?"

"Speaking. Who is this please?"

She heard a sharp intake of breath on the end of the line. "Just listen to me! Damon's escaped from the hospital."

Charlene jolted. This wasn't in her plans. "Who is this? Doctor?"

"No, no. You don't understand. I've found out Danny's contacted Jonny James's killers and he's meeting 'em. They'll be there any time now."

"Oh fuck!" Charlene placed the voice. "Billy. I get you. Promise me one thing – no police. I'll deal with this."

Billy hesitated. "You – how? Ms Monroe – *who are you?*"

Charlene smiled grimly. Good question. "I'll fill you in one day, over dinner." She cleaned the last traces of make-up from her face and was frightened at what she saw, eyes piggy and mean, glaring at her reflection. "Pay attention Billy. I know, and you know, that one of these fellas is a copper don't we?"

"Yerr…" responded Billy forlornly, "he's been stalling the investigation all this time."

"Right. So try and do anything and you'll have the whole force on your back like a mongrel with a hard on, you understand that? Plus another dead kid on your conscience."

"But what're you gonna do?"

"I'm gonna–" Charlene stopped herself mid-sentence. "I'm gonna intercept Damon before they can get to him. Don't worry. After all, I'm just a big girl – what can I do?"

"OK…" Billy sounded doubtful.

"So, where is it all taking place? Quick!"

"The Peace Gardens." Charlene heard a disturbance on the end of the phone line and Billy piped up urgently. "Listen, I'd better go."

"OK, thank you Billy–" The line was already dead, leaving a hiss trickling through the earpiece. Charlene placed the receiver back, slowly.

She breathed deep, collecting her thoughts. Her vast chest rose and fell and she was sure she felt the silicon sloshing around giddily, soothing her with its queasy motion. It was time. She crouched on the floor, searching for her slingbacks. She couldn't go out looking like this, no matter how precious each second was. She had to be properly dressed for the occasion; redo her make-up. Really, she had to admit, she only ever began to enjoy her job since she discovered couture. Finding her shoes, she reached for the bedside cabinet. In the drawer, amongst half-empty bottles of nail varnish remover, was a small cache of firearms – a .45 calibre pistol, a sawn-off shotgun wedged sideways and a sleek automatic. She pulled out the automatic, checked it was loaded, and shoved it down her belt as she lunged for the wardrobe.

The night glimmered with a silvery sheen, the moon a bloated yellow ball sagging just above the rooftops. The air was stock still, swallowing the twilight city noise. Sweat prickled on the nape of Damon's neck, itching his patched up shoulder as he emerged from the hulking shadows of St George's Hall into the two-tiered pathways of the Peace Gardens, a precise interlude in the concrete sprawl and bus lane zigzag. He noted wryly that he was about to implement his own justice in the lap of the city's law courts. He felt so sure of himself that he could have laughed out loud. He began to hum to himself Grace's 'It's Not Over Yet' – disco oblivion, hedonistic empty 4/4s, relentless, perfect pop… These days, what else really mattered?

The town hall clock struck 3.30, its chime muffled by the sluggish air. Damon clammed up. At that precise moment a red Toyota appeared, circling him on the ring road as he looked down. Damon saw three fuzzy figures in their seats, faces upturned towards him. He knew instinctively that these were them – his blood brothers, his partners in crime. He looked forward to seeing them again. Waving cheerfully, he watched their cautious approach.

After a few minutes the Toyota pulled in slowly, coming to rest in front of the Walker Art Gallery some 20 yards away. The driver switched off the engine, but the car headlamps were left beaming onto Damon, hurting his eyes. The figures stepped out warily and, after looking around, began to walk towards him.

As their blurry silhouettes sharpened into familiar monsters, an ache welled in Damon's chest, drawing deep on the buried memories of Jonny's death. He clenched his teeth, determined to override the pain. Deeper, meatier, was the desire to inflict pain himself. He smiled broadly at them, the sides of his mouth smarting.

Only now was he seeing their faces for the first time. Absurdly, he found himself thinking that two were dog ugly, while the youngest one wasn't bad. Blue eyes glittered in a coffee-coloured face; Damon couldn't help but think he resembled a butch Andy Peters. Just his type. Damon's throat felt dry and he swallowed to compensate. He wasn't here to swap phone numbers.

The biggest lad, glistening in an azure shell suit, stepped forward. He looked Damon up and down in disdain. "Right, you got us here. What's this all about?" He looked agitatedly from the pretty boy to the other one, his face rife with terminal acne.

"Thanks fer coming," said Damon dryly.

The spotty lad gobbed onto the ground, looking edgy. "Fuckin' 'ell, let's go! I don't like this one fuckin' bit. Look at 'im, he's so happy with 'imself you think he'd won the lottery."

"Shut it!" warned the pretty boy, sweat prickling his brow.

Damon raised his free arm and they all shrunk from him. "What are you afraid of? A little queer with a busted arm and a black eye? That's a laugh." He took a couple of steps forward, subtly, quickly. "You're wondering why I haven't called the police? Don't get your knickers in a twist. This is just between you and me."

The big lad jabbed a finger at him. "Yer what?" he snorted. "You got any idea what you're dealing with 'ere? This isn't a fuckin' game!"

Damon nodded coolly. "I think I've a pretty good picture what I'm dealing with. That's why I'm not shitting in my pants like you are right now."

He shuffled on his feet, sensing the ground elastic beneath the soles of his Nikes. "Let's see. At least two petty criminals more used to shoplifting than being accessories to murder. Then," pointing to the lad in the shell suit, "one copper's son as bent as his dad – 'scuse the pun – who they say has a great future in organised GBH. If anyone gets to hear what community policing amounts to these days…"

The big lad smiled maliciously. "Look's like the poofter's been doing his homework."

"Like I said, I know who I'm dealing with." Damon edged ever closer. "That's why I know you're more scared of me than I am of you. If you fuck up, you'll have the goons on you like a ton of bricks. If it's hard for me to take you seriously, how are the top brass supposed to?"

The pretty boy started forward and the big lad raised a hand to restrain him. "You're just all talk," he said calmly. "I'm not afraid of you, or them, or anybody."

"So shut the fuck up!" barked the pretty boy. "We should've sorted you like we did your mate."

The big lad nodded, yawning. "Time's up." He cracked his knuckles. "I think this is the perfect chance to correct our mistake."

Damon's eyes narrowed. He took another step towards them. If he reached out his fingers could almost touch them. "Is that right? Tell me then, how's it feel to kill a queer?"

"Yer what?" The spotty lad puckered his face into an ugly ball. "You're a fuckin' nutter."

The big lad grinned, revealing a mouthful of nicotine stained teeth. "I'll tell you what it's like. It's a fuckin' laugh."

"Yeah," chortled the pretty boy shrilly, "it's like putting 'em out of their misery. Doing 'em a favour."

Damon swallowed hard, feeling an icicle thirstily lick his centre. "Queers must do something to really piss you off, eh? To want to do them in like that?" He shook away a trickle of sweat caressing his profile.

The three of them looked at each other hotly. "Your sort fuckin' disgust me!" the big lad spat, his face etched with violence. "Up each other's arses. On the telly. Pretty boys. You should all be rounded up and exterminated along with your filthy diseases. The Krouts had the right idea."

"Yeah, mincing around with carrots up your cunts." The pretty boy went bright red, appearing bothered and perplexed.

Damon stared, aghast, at his aggressors. That was it? It was so inarticulate, so ludicrous, that he burst out laughing.

Three pairs of eyes regarded him uncertainly. "You think it's funny?" asked the big lad.

"I'm laughing at *you,* lard arse!" snapped Damon. He had at least expected a coherent justification for the unjust – but he wasn't going to get it from these gorillas. Jonny's fate was death by turgid heterosexuality. Ignorant, stupid and ugly – it knew no rule book, nor did it respect what it struggled to understand. Damon buckled beneath the sheer weight of it. But he was glad to be gay – the alternative was too horrible to contemplate. And he was happier that Jonny had died a queer rather than lived as a breeder. His mind was made up. "Yeah well," he said dismissively, "I reckon you're all closet fags anyway." Damon's free hand shot under his jacket.

He lunged outwards at their faces, a flash of metal curled around his fingers. The louts stepped back – Damon's action seemed to cut thin air. Visible in his fist as he wavered, a surgical knife, delicate. On seeing that, the big lad sneered, relieved. "Is that the fucking best you can do, bumboy?" Damon looked slowly from them to the exquisite blade. Its tip was laced with red – he had felt it sink in.

The pretty boy dropped to his knees silently, clutching his throat. He began to gurgle. Blood pushed eager through his thick knuckles, pulsing excitedly and flowing down his knees to the ground. The others turned in mute shock to watch him keel over onto his face, his cranium crashing with a sickening thud onto the tatty paving.

"You little…" In white-hot terror the spotty lad took faltering steps back towards the car as the other, his agitated face bursting with blood vessels, pulled a revolver from his jacket. Damon watched him numbly, rooted to the spot. He dropped the blade and lowered his good arm to rest limply at his side.

The homophobe's finger curled around the trigger as he pointed the gun's blunt snout at Damon's face. "The only good queer's a dead queer!" he snarled, his eyes sparkling with animalistic intent, his skin mutating into weird shapes. Damon found himself reflecting on the banality of the remark as he closed his eyes and bowed his head. The sting of a single gunshot rang through the air.

Damon quivered on his feet. The homophobe regarded him incredulously, seemingly as astounded as he was that he was still standing. A clean hole flared in the middle of the thug's forehead. Stuff began to emerge from it and dribble down his nose. He collapsed in a crumpled heap next to his mate.

Damon spun on his heels as he came to his senses. Charlene stood there, resplendent in a suede catsuit. She brushed past him and, pocketing her own pistol, snatched the prone firearm from the homophobe's dead grasp. She held it before her in both hands, one eye closed as she sized up her target, the spotty lad scurrying back to the car. The gun spurted fire with an elegant splishing sound. The lout screeched, clutching his left thigh. He stumbled then continued to drag himself to the vehicle, one leg useless.

Charlene began to walk forward, her long stride swallowing the distance between her and her victim. Sobbing, he heaved himself into the driver's seat, fiddling maniacally at the ignition. The car spluttered into life and he thumped his foot hard on the accelerator. It jerked on the spot as he fumbled the gears. Charlene stood at the open window now, placing the muzzle of the gun against the lad's forehead. "Excuse me, darling." She bent closer and reached for the ignition, switching off the engine with a gloved hand. Suddenly, she did a double take. "Hold on, I'm sure I know you!" she said. "What's your name, love?"

The lad spoke through chattering teeth as the gun nestled between two angry looking yellowheads. "P-Pinky. Pinky McGregor."

"Of course, yes!" Charlene hooted. "Well fuck me, that's a turn up for the books! I knew your dad! McGregor." She sniffed and looked down in disdain at Pinky. "Skinny runt like yourself."

In abject terror Pinky turned his gaze towards her, silently pleading. "That's right!" continued Charlene. "If I remember correctly, he had the scrapyard on the corner of Edge Road, didn't he? Nice little earner. Then he fell back on his protection money, got too big for his boots. I had to see to him myself. Told me to eff off so I put him in his place. Very bad manners."

Pinky's voice stuttered as he spoke. "Me dad was dead a long time ago. They said it was Charlie Monroe that did it. The police never found him. Thought he'd been bumped off too – found his Jag in the Mersey and all."

Charlene nodded fervently. "Your memory's better than mine, Perky love. But no, Charlie Monroe wasn't bumped off, it just looked that way. I'll admit, he came pretty close to getting caught."

"What – what yer mean?"

Charlene paused. She removed the gun from Pinky's temple and he almost wet himself with relief. Charlene didn't notice. Her expression was indefinable as she reflected on lost indian summers. Maybe though, beneath the heavy mascara, her contacts were tinged with sadness. "See if this one rings any bells. Charlie used to play with you when you were growing up, remember that Perky? He and your dad were big mates. He used to bounce you up and down on his knee." Charlene began to stroke the homophobe along the length of his temple with her gloved hand. "You used to always go on about his tattoo, on his right forearm. Remember what the tattoo was?"

The spotty lad frowned, looking confused. "A – spider. A black widow spider."

Charlene jammed the gun back against the homophobe's forehead as she began to role up the sleeve of her catsuit. "I was going to have it removed when I had my boobs done," she said airily, "but I knew I would regret it one day." She brandished her forearm before the boy. His eyes widened as he recognised the tattoo crawling up her slender wrist, identical, if faded, after three decades. "Charlie Monroe might be dead," she announced, "but Charlene Monroe is very much alive and pissed off." She flicked the safety catch resolutely. "I don't mind telling you Perky, your dad was partial to a bit of cock himself when no one was looking." Charlene smiled serenely. "They say size isn't everything, but believe me, he had nothing to complain about."

Pinky began to emit a low, strangled moan as he seared Charlene with his eyes. Her pristine, smug face was the last thing he saw. She pressed the trigger and his head bounced as his brains splattered against the mustard upholstery in a riot of colour. A crater the size of a clenched fist hissed in his cranium, expelling bilge. The lad's torso thrashed briefly before toppling forward and clunking against the dashboard.

Charlene breathed deep and pulled her revolver from her pocket. Juggling two guns in her hands like a pro, she wiped her firearm with a flourish. She placed it in the clenched fist of the dead driver, arranging his arm so that it hung awkward out of the window. "Hardly perfect, but the police will get the idea I'm sure," she said. "Another gangland killing." She looked impassively from the carnage to Damon, who stared at her snagged between euphoria and horror. "Charlene, I—"

"Spare me!" she snapped. "Where's the scalpel? What the hell were you expecting to do with that?"

Damon felt a cold needle dance down his spine, as he pointed to the blade lying lamely on the ground. The enormity of his actions crept up on him; three inert corpses lay smarting like sores on the pavement of Liverpool city centre. He looked up into the black sky, wondering if their spirits hovered above, observing their lives ebbing away. The sky confronted him balefully. He shivered. "I don't know. I did it for Jonny. I didn't care what happened to me afterwards."

Charlene paused and cupped Damon's face in her hands. Her expression softened. She kissed him softly on the lips – he quivered like a chaste kitten. "Sweetheart, I care. Your friends care." She strode over to the body of the man with brain matter seeping onto the pavement and curled his fingers around the remaining pistol, taking care to remove her own prints. Then, dipping into her pocket, she unearthed a mobile phone. She motioned for quiet, rapidly dialling a local number.

"Sergeant Ivanosec? Sorry to get you out of bed. How is young Danny, still giving value for money? Good, send him my love. I'll get to the point. The Jonny James case? I've done you a big favour by solving it. Send a squad car to the Peace Gardens and you'll see what I mean. And an ambulance.

Uh–huh. I don't expect to hear another word on this matter, of course. Thank you Sergeant. Glad to be of help." Charlene rung off.

Damon's eyes bulged in awe. "That's it?"

Charlene nodded. "That's it." She put an arm around Damon's shoulders. "Let's get a cab, shall we?"

Damon wobbled on his feet. "I feel sick."

Charlene indicated the shrubbery. "I bet you do, love. Go on, bring it all up. I'll dispose of the knife in one of the 'Pool's sweet-smelling drains."

Damon barely managed to stagger over to the undergrowth before he retched, feeling the evil rise in his gorge and out into the balmy summer air. Tears mingled with his vomit dripping onto the shrubs in thick bubbles, flowing so easily. He couldn't tell whether it was his wretched stomach or real pain that made him cry, and he never would know for sure.

As Charlene helped him down the steps of St George's Hall, a milk cart trundled laboriously across the bus lane. Charlene waved cheerily at the Rastafarian driver, who grinned broadly on seeing her. "Ms Charlene. What are you doing up so early in the morning?"

She shrugged. "Just killing time, Oswald."

The milk cart glided past them, the driver craning his neck to wave goodbye. "Give 'em one for me, Ms Charlene… Have a nice day." His voice was swallowed by the high-rise.

"From now on, I plan to," she said emphatically. "Come on Damon, it's really over."

Epilogue

THE MORNING WAS CRISP AND CLEAR, nature threatening to make headway in the bricks and mortar. The ten thirty-five sun bathed the pretty Georgian terraces in golden arcs as an insistent breeze whipped up the soft carpet of autumn leaves. Gus banged the front door shut, breathing deeply in the aromatic chill, feeling the soft plant mush clog his heels as he stepped into the street. His nasal passages relented, air whooshing down his windpipe where previously he would have snorted thick snot into his brain before being able to breathe. It felt good to be so – *clear.* Gus was officially two weeks substance-free.

As he shuffled down the road towards the paper shop, he took note of a 'For Rent' placard swaying before the recently renovated flats off Huskisson Street. The beleaguered lads who had felt the brunt of gay pride didn't even dare to pack their own bags before leaving for a safer – straighter – part of town. Gus had watched their families troop in and out with furniture and boxes; they had looked disappointingly harmless. Gus didn't know whether he expected to recognise some gay-hating gene etched into their faces – rather he saw respectability, colour co-ordination and a near-robotic precision in their bland middle class aura.

Gus came to and said a quick queer prayer for Damon – a daily ritual. While his friend had managed to side-step the shock waves generated following the Peace Gardens' massacre, Charlene nevertheless felt that Damon should ride out the controversy with tranny mates in Berlin. Gus and Serge had said sleepy-headed goodbyes to their buddy that

179

night, awoken by an urgent phone call. Then Damon was off to Lowestoft to catch the first Ostend ferry before sunrise. Gus hadn't heard a thing since, but he had to assume no news was good news.

Liverpool, in the meantime, had become reassuringly aggro-free – the latest incidents he knew of centred on Canal Street in Manchester, as groups of straight lads began to besiege the Gay Village with broken bottles and flick knives. Gus wondered if the authorities couldn't just have them put down or something? Well, he was sorry, but this was one problem Manchester was going to have to sort out without his help.

Maybe they should do themselves a favour and send for Charlene and her polysexual heavies. The last Gus heard, she was out with the Chanel glitz and in with a sleek gangsta profile. One time, Gus was meandering back home from the chippie when a black limo, sheer as a torpedo, drew up before him and blocked his path, engine throbbing. Gus's hackles rose, but as he scrutinised the dense velvet of the blinded glass, he sensed that behind it a friend, not foe, was looking right back. He never saw his suspicions confirmed, but he was sure Charlene observed him before being driven off, accelerating into the sunset. And that was it. She had left the boys well alone since Damon's departure, and taken the bad karma with her.

Autumn 1996 was threatening to be radically anti-climactic. Gus was up to the challenge, he thought, all demons exorcised though his looks still scared little kids and jittery OAPs. There were compromises he wouldn't make for anyone, not even Serge. His hair was cobalt blue now, while he was booked in next week to have his cock pierced. Wryly, he recalled as a kid his mam's weekly hair appointment for a shampoo and set. My, how times change! Yesterday, his folks had invited him around for tea, but Gus was more excited about the prospect of having a ring stabbed through the head of his penis.

Serge affected disapproval but Gus knew that, on the sly, he was fascinated. Their obvious differences proved as stimulating as they were unavoidable – it was the key to their relationship. Gus persevered, digging ever deeper, but he felt himself thudding against an unyielding stone core and he knew this was where the real Serge hid. Patience. All he could do was chip at it doggedly. In fact, while Serge had softened Gus's hard edges, Gus was delighted to have brought out in Serge an unexpected desire to be blown while tied to the home furnishings. He would come so fiercely in Gus's mouth that he was sure the spunk dribbled out of his ears.

"Hello Mr Anwar!" chirped Gus breezily.

The paper shop owner looked at him over his National Health bifocals before breaking into a broad grin. "Hello Gus. For a moment I didn't recognise you there. Blue. Nice colour."

"Thanks a lot." He skimmed the magazine rack, pulling out *Elle* and flicking through it briefly. "I'm not reading it, I promise," he said. He dropped it onto the counter and looked over Mr Anwar's shoulder, squinting. "I'll have a couple of those fancy pens too, the pink ones." He pointed and, as Mr Anwar turned unwittingly, stuffed a Lion Bar into his trousers. The shopkeeper swivelled to face him while scrutinising the price tag on the pens, blissfully unaware of the chocolate bar shoved into Gus's pocket. He rang up the items on the till. "That's four pound twenty."

Gus started. Fucking expensive pens! It would have been cheaper to buy the Lion Bar. But dull dull dull. As he grudgingly fished out four one pound coins, he commiserated that he couldn't visit his local paper shop without nicking something, particularly since he was heading for unashamed domesticity with the Boy Wonder. Gus went off down the road, whistling.

His world glittered prettily as he took a detour to Sharma's place. 'Wannabe' battered his eardrums from the slightly open bay window, shaking the street's foundations. It was on the radio, on Katy Ann's hi-fi, *everywhere*. He liked it. He rang the doorbell.

Katy Ann came down and answered the door in dungarees and a vintage Seditionaries Destroy T-shirt. She looked sulky.

"Hiya gorgeous," said Gus. "You like the Spice Girls then?"

"Uh-huh," answered Katy Ann curtly. "Mam's still in bed. She's with that fella from Cream again."

Gus looked at her sympathetically. "Don't think much of him, do yer?"

Katy Ann sniffed. "He's not my cup of tea." She suddenly looked twice her age.

Gus pulled out a pen from his pocket. "I got you a prezzie. You still drawing comics?" Katy Ann brightened, nodding. "Ta. Uncle Gus, can I come and play at your flat with you and Uncle Serge?"

"Sure. Just leave a note for your mum, eh?"

She spun on her heels excitedly. "Affirmative!"

Gus ushered Katy Ann into his bedsit, where she immediately launched herself at the sofa and began fiddling with the TV remote. "Hi honey, I'm home!" hollered Gus. "I've brought chocolate and a young girl for us to have our wicked way with."

Katy Ann stuck her tongue out, eyeing the Lion Bar as Gus dropped it onto the coffee table. "Geroff that," he said, "it's for my beau."

The little girl returned her attention to the TV screen. "Got any crisps?"

"We do." From the bathroom Gus heard Serge's muffled voice. "I'm in the bath." The plug hiccuped and water gloop-glooped down the hole.

Gus emptied a packet of Cheesie Wotsits into a Tupperware and placed them before Katy Ann. "Isn't your mother feeding you?" he asked disparagingly. She ignored his remark as she grabbed a handful of crisps and wolfed them down. "Look Uncle Gus," she said, between mouthfuls, "it's *The Chart Show*. You want to watch?"

Gus came and sat beside her on the sofa, cuddling Katy Ann in his arms. "I don't know," he remarked, "I've lost all track since falling in love."

Katy Ann nodded in mute seriousness. As they concentrated on the onslaught of frenetic video imagery, Serge emerged into the lounge clad solely in a bath towel. "Hiya darling. Hiya Katy Ann." They resolutely ignored the lush display of dripping flesh, voluptuous in its curves, generous in the milky helpings of porcelain smoothness. His hummingbird tattoo shone like new. Popping on Serge's chin was a nebulous froth of shaving foam.

"Hiya Serge, how are you, light of my life?" he said to himself sarcastically, looking askance at his oblivious audience. "Fine, thank you Gus," he continued. "Nice you ask."

"Sssh!" hissed Gus, jabbing a forefinger in the direction of the screen. "Telly."

Serge nodded short-temperedly, peering at the television garble. He felt the shaving foam begin to contract on his chin. "Did you get my razor blades the other day?"

Gus indicated his satchel vaguely. "Uh-huh. You'll find them in there." He focused again on the television, running a hand through Katy Ann's soft hair.

Serge, grumbling quietly to himself at Gus's indifference, delved deep into the bag. He peered inside with a look of faint revulsion. "Jesus, what have you got in here?" His arm was swallowed up to the elbow as he rummaged around gingerly.

Gus looked up, slightly irritable. "It's all the love letters and gifts from my many lovers—" He froze as he witnessed Serge pull out a tatty envelope from the recesses of the bag, frowning as he recognised his name. "This is for me." He looked from the letter to Gus. "How long have you had this?" His face betrayed ill-concealed dismay. He scrutinised the postmark. "This letter's a couple of months old…"

Katy Ann caught the scent of trouble and looked up. Gus had gone stark white, like the sudden dazzle of dark to light. "Fucking 'ell Serge," he stammered, "I'd forgotten it was even there." He pulled himself out of the sofa and stepped forward.

Serge kept him at arm's length as he began to read the contents of the moth-eaten letter. A myriad of emotions flickered across his face; he looked up at Gus, wounded. "How could you – keep this from me?" Tears glistened at the ducts.

Gus grimaced. "I didn't Serge!" he pleaded. "It's just with everything that happened."

"Don't even bother!" Serge pushed past Gus and made for the smalls drawer. "Katy Ann, you go home," he said steadily.

The little girl jumped to her feet. "Can I take the crisps with me?" she asked quickly. Gus nodded and herded her to the front door. "Go straight home, eh?" He looked scared to death.

Katy Ann nodded affirmative and pulled the door behind her. As her footsteps rang down the stairs, in the bedsit a tense hush descended.

Serge, dry now, was stepping into a pair of Calvin Klein briefs that moulded perfectly to the contours of his arse. Gus watched him grab his clothes from the wardrobe. "What're you doing?" he asked nervously.

"I have to go. My family needs me."

"Don't be daft!" Gus yelped. "You can't go, just like that!" Colour raced to his face and his heart clattered loudly like a pneumatic drill.

Serge threw him a venomous glance. "Watch me." He pursed his lips before saying any more and began stuffing his clothes into a backpack pulled from under the bed.

"I'll come with you!" blurted out Gus impulsively.

Serge shook his head. "You would be a nuisance. You're as ready for a Bosnian winter as for a proper haircut."

Gus felt idiotic. "What – what's the letter say?"

"My sisters are disappeared. The village say it was a Serbian army patrol crossing the border. They will be lucky to be alive – if we can find them."

"Jesus Christ." Gus collapsed inward. "Oh Serge, I'm so sorry, but–"

Serge cut him short. "It's too late to be sorry." He looked at Gus fiercely. "Maybe you thought that if you hide my letters from me, you would be able to control me. Charlene thought so too. Big mistake."

Gus averted his eyes. "P'raps at the beginning that were true Serge, but I honestly forgot it were there a long time ago. Please believe me!"

Serge shrugged casually. "It make no difference now if I believe you or not." He bent down to tie his bootlaces. "I always knew this wouldn't work between us," he added maliciously.

"That so?" Gus went bright crimson and muttered something under his breath. Serge cocked his head to one side querulously. "What did you say?"

"Nothing."

"Tell me what you said!"

Gus stiffened. "I said – I love you."

The boy was taken aback, staring agog at Gus.

"Yeah," Gus continued, "I won't make a scene 'cos you're going. I also understand why you're pissed off with me and you're right, I never wanted yer to leave. But let's just get one thing straight, Serge – things were working out just fine. Don't you dare make out otherwise."

Serge grimaced and turned his back on Gus. "I'll get my toothbrush."

Gus felt a rush of irritation rise unaided through him. "Yeah, it's like you couldn't wait to bugger off," he said bitterly. He picked up the Lion Bar and threw it at Serge. "I got you something for the journey." He watched Serge pocket it, before re-emerging from the bathroom clutching a few toiletries. Serge stuffed them down the side of his rucksack and heaved it over his broad shoulders, sagging under the weight. "Well," he grunted, "that's everything. I send you a postcard."

Gus bit his lip savagely. "As if I'm fussed."

Serge winced. "OK. I'll see you." He brushed by Gus, head bowed. As he reached the front door he turned, aware of Gus's gaze burning into the back of his head. Their eyes crashed messily. Serge exited without another word.

Gus held his breath, praying that Serge might burst in and gather him into his arms again, smothering him in repentant kisses. He strained his hearing, fiddling nervously with his knuckles. Serge stomped down the stairs, puffing, before banging the heavy front door behind him.

Gus clutched his cobalt blue hair and yanked himself to his feet. From the window he saw Serge hail a black cab, hurtling down Canning Street to the city centre. The taxi screeched to a halt melodramatically. Serge's bulging rucksack was chucked into the boot and the beer-bellied driver held the passenger door open for his client, evidently enthralled to have a lucrative fare to Manchester Airport. Gus stared down fixedly, anxious that Serge should look up at the window. The Bosnian boy, as big as Gus's hand, slipped straight onto the back seat and the cab drove off, taking Serge downtown into the steely bite of autumn's chill.

Gus turned away and flopped onto the bed. He drew his knees up to his chest and began to rock silently. He closed his eyes, and behind his vision his head swam eerily violet. All he heard, as he balanced there on the bed end, was the howl of a speeding police car, heading towards Toxteth. Gus sank down into the duvet, still clutching his legs in the ghost of an ultrasound scan, fuzzy and hard to decipher. He felt heavy as lead. He lay there, just so.

CODEX

CRUCIFY ME AGAIN • Mark Manning

ISBN: 1 899598 14 6 • £8.95UK • $14.50USA • $22.95AUS/CAN

For a decade Mark Manning was Zodiac Mindwarp, sex god, love machine from outer space and frontman of heavy metal band The Love Reaction. *Crucify Me Again* documents the spiralling depravity of his years within the moral quagmire of bad sex, worse drugs and truly horrific rock and roll. Presenting a vivid series of incidents from his life, Mark Manning explores parts of his psyche most people would rather believe didn't exist.

Mark Manning has worked extensively with Bill Drummond of The KLF, co-authoring *Bad Wisdom* and the 'Bad Advice' column for *The Idler*.

'Tales of excess and bravado imbued with a self-deprecating wit'
— The Guardian

CHARLIEUNCLENORFOLKTANGO • Tony White

ISBN: 1 899598 13 8 • £7.95UK • $11.95USA • $19.95AUS/CAN

CHARLIEUNCLENORFOLKTANGO is a 'stream-of-sentience' alien abduction cop novel, the bastard offspring of *Starsky and Hutch* and *The X Files*.

CHARLIEUNCLENORFOLKTANGO is the call sign of three English cops driving around in a riot van. Problem is, one of these cops is not entirely human. The Sarge thinks it's him, and Lockie — the narrator — thinks he's right. In between witnessing and committing various atrocities and acts of work-a-day corruption, and being experimented on by aliens, Lockie thinks aloud about old Blakie and The Sarge, cave blokes and cave birds and *Charlie's Angels*.

Tony White has published two novels, *Road Rage* and *Satan Satan Satan!* and edited the *britpulp!* anthology.

'Utterly brutal, darkly hilarious — the most remarkable novel of alien abduction I've ever read' — Front

DIGITAL LEATHERETTE • Steve Beard
ISBN: 1 899598 12 X • £8.95UK • $14.50USA • $22.95AUS/CAN

Digital Leatherette is a surrealist narrative pulled down from invented web-sites by an imaginary intelligent agent. The ultimate London cypherpunk novel features: the Rave at the End of the World; street riots sponsored by fashion designers; a stellar-induced stock market crash; the new drug, Starflower, and barcode tattoos.

Steve Beard is the author of *Logic Bomb* and *Perfumed Head*. He has written for magazines including *i-D* and *The Face*.

'An exuberant, neurologically-specific, neo-Blakeian riff-collage. I enjoyed it enormously'
                                                        – William Gibson

CONFUSION INCORPORATED: A Collection of Lies, Hoaxes & Hidden Truths • Stewart Home
ISBN: 1 899598 11 1 • £7.95UK • $11.95USA • $19.95AUS/CAN

Confusion Incorporated brings together, for the first time, the hilarious journalistic deceptions of arch wind-up merchant Stewart Home. This collection is imaginative, complicated, subtle and funny – very, very funny. Regardless of whether Home is being crude, rude or devious, he hits his targets with deadly accuracy and side-splitting effect.

Stewart Home is the author of numerous books including *The Assault On Culture* and *Blow Job*. He has contributed journalism to an astonishing range of newspapers, magazines and fanzines.

'Quick, funny – the outrageous pieces leap off the page with manic energy'
                                                        – Time Out

CRANKED UP REALLY HIGH • Stewart Home
ISBN: 1 899598 01 4 • £5.95UK • $9.50USA • $14.95AUS/CAN

A lot of ink has been spilt on the subject of punk rock in recent years, most of it by arty-farty trendies who want to make the music intellectually respectable. *Cranked Up Really High* is different. It isn't published by a university press and it gives short shrift to the idea that the roots of punk rock can be traced back to 'avant garde' art movements.

'A complex, provocative book which deserves to be read'   – Mojo

"i'd rather you lied"
Selected Poems 1980-1998 • Billy Childish

ISBN: 1 899598 10 3 • £9.95UK • $17.95USA • $24.95AUS/CAN

Selected from over 30 published collections, *"i'd rather you lied"* brings together a life-time's work of one of the most remarkable and unorthodox voices of the late twentieth century. Accompanied by woodcuts and drawings from now rare or unobtainable originals, this volume sees Billy Childish take his rightful place as the poet laureate of the underdog.

A legendary figure in underground writing, painting and music, Billy Childish has published more than 30 collections of poetry and two novels, recorded over 80 albums and exhibited his paintings worldwide.

'His poems are raw, unmediated, bruisingly shocking in their candour and utter lack of sentimentality' – Daily Telegraph

NOTEBOOKS OF A NAKED YOUTH
Billy Childish

ISBN: 1 899598 08 1 • £7.95UK • $19.95AUS • Not available in the USA

Highly personal and uncompromising, *Notebooks of a Naked Youth* is narrated by one William Loveday, an acned youth possessed of piercing intelligence, acute self-loathing and great personal charm. Haunted by intense sexual desires, the ghosts of his childhood and a 7000 year old mummified Bog Man, William Loveday leads us on a naked odyssey from the 'Rust Belt' of North Kent to the sleazy sex clubs of Hamburg's Reeperbahn – a twilight world of murderous pimps and tattooed hermaphrodites – and a final descent into an expressionist hell.

In this, his 'fantastic biography', Billy Childish achieves the unholy union of punk rock, Knut Hamsun and Céline. The result is a hilarious, drunken, un-English voyage into the human shadow. *Notebooks of a Naked Youth* is the powerful sequel to *My Fault,* Childish's first novel.

'Childish spits out vicious literary disgust in great gobbets of rancour' –The Big Issue

SATAN'S SLAVES • Richard Allen

New Introduction by Stewart Home
ISBN: 1 899598 07 3 • £6.95UK • $10.50USA

'There is plenty here to satisfy those who crave the spectacle of outrage and horror' – Stewart Home

Satan's Slaves is a vivid account of drop-out sixties California. Allen fingers hippie cult leader Charles Manson as living proof that straight society has been abandoned by an entire generation and attempts to throw light upon the evil that culminated in The Family slayings.

Seventies pulp writer Richard Allen, is notorious for violent exploitation skinhead novels such as *Boot Boys* and *Suedehead*.

PSYCHOBOYS • Bertie Marshall

ISBN: 1 899598 05 7 • £5.95UK • $9.50USA

Set in the cities of Moscow and Berlin, *Psychoboys* tells the story of Rez, a rent boy living on the streets, and his fight for survival in a world of bizarre strangers. He meets a riot of characters: Ms Thing, a transvestite sugar mummy, who educates him in the art of coprophilia and barbiturate abuse and leads him into sex and death trips; Countess Handover, a drag-queen genetic engineer who offers Rez the 'gift' of a lifetime; and The Lost Sailor, Rez's nemesis, who delivers an apocalyptic warning.

Bertie Marshall was born in London, and was one of The Bromley Contingent, the first group of Sex Pistols fans.

'A dark, twisted, deliciously funny little book' – Time Out

FLICKERS OF THE DREAMACHINE • Paul Cecil (ed)

ISBN: 1 899598 03 0 • £7.95UK • $11.95USA

Devised in the early sixties by artist Brion Gysin and mathematician Ian Sommerville, the Dreamachine is still the simplest and most effective of all brain-wave stimulators. Notable users include William Burroughs, Derek Jarman and Kurt Cobain.

Flickers includes construction plans and essays by Gysin and Sommerville, along with artists including Genesis P-Orridge and Ira Cohen.

THE VOIDOID • Richard Hell
ISBN: 1 899598 02 2 • £5.95UK • $7.95USA

"*The Voidoid* was written in 1973 in a little furnished room on East 10th Street. Every day I'd take a cheap bottle of wine with me across the street to the $16-a-week room I'd rented for writing. Sometimes afterwards if I had some extra money I'd go the pharmacy on Second Avenue and buy a bottle of codeine cough syrup and come back and lie on the cot again…"

Hell is best known for the proto-punk classics 'Blank Generation' and 'Love Comes In Spurts'.

CODEX PERFORMANCE
Original performances from leading contemporary writers on CD

BROUGHT TO LIGHT • Alan Moore & Gary Lloyd
ISBN: 1 899598 56 1 • 67 minutes • £9.95UK • $18.99USA
A disturbingly vivid mix of conspiracy and menacing soundscapes.

THE BRIDGE • Iain Banks & Gary Lloyd
ISBN: 1 899598 57 X • 43 minutes • £9.95UK • $18.99USA
A stunning audio experience, much more than a talking book.

GO NOW • Richard Hell
ISBN: 1 899598 53 7 • 21 minutes • £7.95UK • $14.95USA
Leading light of the New York punk scene reads his story of a musician down on his luck.

PUSSY • Kathy Acker
ISBN: 1 899598 52 9 • 60 minutes • £9.95UK • $18.99USA
Bursting with graphic sex, wanton plagiarism and a persuasive worldview of visionary subversion.

HEXENTEXTS – A Creation Books Sampler
ISBN: 1 899598 51 0 • 62 minutes • £7.95UK • $14.95USA
Words and music from the cutting edge of Creation's list.

To order, send a cheque, postal order or IMO (payable to CODEX, in Pounds Sterling, drawn on a British bank) to **Codex, PO Box 148, Hove, BN3 3DQ, UK.** Postage is free in the UK, add £1 per item for Europe, £2 for the rest of the world. Send a stamp (UK) or International Reply Coupon for a full list of available books and CDs.
Website: www.codexbooks.co.uk • Email: codex@codexbooks.co.uk